NONE BUT THE RIGHTEOUS

NONE
BUT THE
RIGHTEOUS

A NOVEL

Chantal James

COUNTERPOINT

Berkeley, California

None but the Righteous

Library of Congress Cataloging-in-Publication Data
Names: James, Chantal, 1985– author.
Title: None but the righteous : a novel / Chantal James.
Description: First hardcover edition. | Berkeley, California : Counterpoint,
    2022.
Identifiers: LCCN 2021001525 | ISBN 9781640094598 (hardcover) | ISBN
    9781640094604 (ebook)
Subjects: LCSH: Psychological fiction.
Classification: LCC PS3610.A4286 N66 2022 | DDC 813/.6—dc23
LC record available at https://lccn.loc.gov/2021001525

Jacket design by Dana Li
Book design by Jordan Koluch

COUNTERPOINT
2560 Ninth Street, Suite 318
Berkeley, CA 94710
www.counterpointpress.com

Printed in the United States of America

10 9 8 7 6 5 4 3 2 1

For Vivian Rouson and Nadia Jai,
old and new quarters of the city

CONTENTS

I. WHAT IS FALLEN

II. WHAT IS RESTORED

III. WHAT IS REDEEMED

I.

WHAT IS FALLEN

1. In which Ham finds alternate homes

When I get so lonesome for the life of the body that the thinnest slice of it will do, I start answering to names that might not otherwise turn my head. Thirsting for the earthly body, I might even stoop to drink liquor left at a crossroads for hoodoo gods, so happy to be bound up again in the cares of the flesh that I hardly care whose flesh it is.

May Ham never wander far enough to know this. His body sits on a bus; his mind wanders back to wonder why he never had a place in Atlanta.

One morning in Atlanta—a place growing further in time and space behind him by the moment while he shuttles ever homeward on a bus with many others—Ham drifted out onto the porch of Mayfly's duplex to have his coffee and view the world through the steam that rose over the brim of the cup. He and

I watched eerie yellows spread stain-like over each tree in view,
turning the street golden as the early sun poured over it. If he
squinted, Ham could see to where the strip of houses ended on
one side at the parking lot of Yassin's Fish. A small figure made
its way toward him from that direction, crossing under the metal
signpost that held Yassin's marquee high above the waking world.
The figure drew closer to Ham, growing in size through the rippled air above his coffee cup, until he could see its female form—a
young woman in a hoodie, walking a bicycle alongside her. Before
long, he could hear the click of the revolutions of the wheels, and
then he could make out Mayfly's furrowed, concentrated expression. He could see the bunch of tough-looking plants with small
purple flowers that she gripped against the bicycle's handlebars.

A few yards away from him, she noticed the vapor that as-
cended from his cup, and, connecting the cup to the hand that
held it, to the shape that could belong to no one but Ham at this
hour, she waved brightly. By the time she'd reached the bottom
of the porch stairs, she'd broken into a smile. "Good morning."

She had been around the block to gather a few plants from
a neighbor's garden to transplant for her own use. Ham smelled
them before he could eye them up close. When the scent hit
him—lavender—he seemed split for a moment into two, leaping
out of himself. Next thing he could remember he was in the living
room with Mayfly, in the middle of a conversation with her. He
heard the words come out of him, he followed these words, he
entered them and was at one with himself again.

The scent of lavender sends Ham jumping out of his body,
the smell of the soap Father Maughn must have used long ago

impressed in his deepest fibers, the smell that cleaved like a film to the man's skin. (The smell Ham could never wash off himself, that memory sends in a vapor from his own pores when he least suspects.)

I think I watch Ham so closely because he knows so well what it is to vacate the body—he has learned how to escape himself, a lesson that death offers freely but that only a privileged, burdened few can grasp before then. I can tell you that as easily as Ham drifts off to undiscovered worlds when this one is too strange to bear, I could drift, even in life. I could split my body in two. My body could be touched, seen, heard in two places at once, appear in deserts across the ocean as solidly as in my hometown, that ancient city peopled by indigenous ghosts—but that is another story, for another hour.

For now, it suffices that Ham and the rest of the road-jostled weary rattle on, shaken from sleep or nostalgia to the same jarring rhythm as the tires of this bus traveling away from Atlanta impact a road in disrepair. Ham's seat partner is a little girl, her fat braids bound by barrettes in the shape of bright plastic globes. Her mother and a brother occupy the row ahead, the mother fanning herself with a magazine. Now and then a puff of the air she has stirred floats back to Ham, whose sticky skin receives it gratefully. Fields of cotton roll past the window, flecks of cloud-white hidden in dark brambles spread and tumbling before an open sky. Down from Atlanta the world heats itself slowly. Winter sloughs off like old skin. The thin air thickens. Time begins to draw itself out, each second pulled fuller than the last.

His seatmate eats from a bag of cheese puffs, and the sound

they make as they are crushed between her tiny teeth turns Ham's head toward her. This inspires the child to offer him some of her snack with fingers coated in a neon orange powder that adheres steadfastly to her skin, staining it. Ham declines.

He slides his palm to the back of his neck, to the tender knot there. He has been sleeping on it badly for so long; on a sofa or a floor at Mayfly's house, where he'd finally managed to arrive at the end of so many dreamlike days after the hurricane, days when it seemed that from sunup he crawled over rocky ground on hands and knees, stumbled until he found somewhere to lay down again by night.

The age gap of eight years between him and Mayfly seemed to have narrowed between the time that had passed since they'd last seen each other until he washed up at her door in Atlanta, storm swept. Ham's words had whistled over the top of Mayfly's head when she met him at her door, and as they'd settled onto opposite ends of her stained yellow sofa it was as equals, with an ease that belied the seven years since they'd last been in the same room.

He'd found her with shorn hair. He remembered Mayfly's hair as a chaotic mass of half-dreads and abandoned knots. It had been a world, that head of hair, with its own ecosystem—a crumb would fall from it, then an insect. Now it lay curled so close to the scalp that the skin showed through. There were other changes: she no longer rode trains; she no longer scavenged for food and clothes in dumpsters, no longer took up residence in abandoned buildings where the figures of the other people squatting there might appear as phantoms around a corner, where the floorboards of the story above creaked as easily from imagined footsteps as from real ones. She now paid rent every month to live in one half of a slightly run-down duplex on a green and shady street, and she went to work five days a week at a call center, soliciting the unsuspecting in the most measured and mellow and courteous of voices, breaking her smooth, deliberate calm only to cuss back at those who cussed her on calls, and then only barely, so that the shock of the raging expletives delivered in such a controlled tone stayed all day with those on the other end of the line.

Half the changes in her, maybe more than half, Ham could not measure. He couldn't observe her from any kind of fixed perspective. He wasn't the little boy he had been when they'd left off, nor was she the taller teenager, and he could not return to a younger form any more than she could. So he wondered if maybe she was only a yardstick by which to measure his own progression; he was useless at coming to these kinds of conclusions.

The child in the seat at his side now draws a deep breath, exactly what Ham feels like doing, and he takes vicarious relief from it. Beyond the highway, through the window, Ham sees the ragged half of a near-demolished building. Its front torn off as if by a giant's fingers, it looks like a dollhouse—its walls cut away to reveal desks, chairs, doorways with miniature doors fluttering in them, half-hallways. Ham's mind's eye, and mine, begins to arrange doll-people inside it, to conjure ghostly doll-lives for them.

In Atlanta, Ham was not nursed. Maybe he'd been hoping for someone to patch up his new wounds, help bridge the canyons that trauma had raised in him when the storm had so brutally severed him from all he'd known. He certainly didn't find that in Atlanta. But he had, in those weeks, recovered some necessary habits: the habit of waking in the same room every morning, a room whose every detail was reassuring; the habit of knowing that if he was hungry there was food in the refrigerator; the habit of seeing, once or twice a day, a face he had known for years. Mayfly did not seem to have many friends, but Ham had met a few of them. One young man, Mayfly's age, with a face so beautiful Ham ached to look at it, the same piercing ache of a cavity as hard candy dissolves to nothing in the mouth. A couple of women, each coming alone to sit and talk. They were a generation or two older than Mayfly and Ham, who were still at the beginning of adulthood. Mayfly kept a garden in pots on her porch, some herbs for cooking and some marigolds and some heliotrope. She watered these every day. She had a beautiful waxy orchid growing in a pot in her kitchen, and she would come to stroke its branches now and then as she moved around the house. She had a canary in a cage in the kitchen, whose sharp little peeps lent the same quality to the space as a ticking clock or a fire alarm that chirped, in need of a new battery.

Ham didn't feel like a burden. He knew that Mayfly didn't expect him to stay forever but that she would have been indifferent if he had. She would have continued to see about him in her perfunctory way, watering him like she watered her plants, feeding him at her table the same way she dropped seeds into a plastic cup for the bird. And in truth Ham would not have asked for any better treatment than to be taken as part of the usual landscape. It was better than being handled as a curiosity or a tragedy.

The only mission he really had was to find some sugarcane for me so he could gnaw all the sweet juice from its fibers and keep my voice near. He feels these urges come from beyond him, urges he knows are not his urges but my urges, the urges whose satisfaction allow him to escape himself in the ways he needs to when the world closes in. He found some one day at a shop owned by some West Africans in the neighborhood.

Mayfly hardly asked him any questions about himself the first week, until one rare evening when Ham was not wandering the streets like a walking dead man, feeling completely apart from the world of the living faces he passed, when she was not out somewhere Ham was not invited. An evening storm had trapped them together in the house like two insects under the dome of an overturned sugar bowl, and they sat together, listening to rain beat at the window, watching it cast underwater shadows on the living room's blue walls. Mayfly shuffled a deck of cards in her hands, not having yet announced what game they were playing, and as she turned to him and parted her lips, he thought she would ask, "Gin rummy or spit?"

Instead she said, "Did you leave much behind?"

The rain's patter could sometimes be mistaken for the rattle of cicadas. Both sounds rose into the air like scent and hung there.

Ham wanted to say "Everything," but what he said was "Not much. I'd just started working on a fishing boat." He thought of the lake's waters and how abundant they were at their best, how provident and merciful and full of life.

"What fish?"

"Grouper and trout. The man who owned the boat was from

around here." A man who'd grown up landlocked, whose boy-hood nose had itched for breezes cast off an ocean, or, failing that, a good, broad, muddy river, or, at the very least, a reservoir vast enough that he couldn't see to its other shore.

"You lived on your own?"

"I'm not a kid," Ham insisted, as though it answered the question.

Mayfly had the posture of someone who gave nothing away, no matter what she searched out and found in the world. If Ham assumed that this stance was something new in her, something that had developed after they'd parted, a second look would have proved otherwise. This was something that had always been with her before she had given up traveling, this unwillingness to yield. It was the same quality that had allowed her to perch atop swift-moving freight trains in the rush of night among strangers who concealed who knew what knives and what rage. It was the dark of night itself, her cloak. Ham was always granted a peek beneath it, and now he turned the hard edge of interrogation toward her to ask abruptly, "How did you feel when you cut your hair?"

Mayfly smiled at the question. "At first I felt like a boy," she said. "Then I felt so light and so cool. It's like years and years fall-ing down at your feet. Like being free from history. And I keep it this way because it makes me feel free."

"I can see that," said Ham, because agreeing was easy. But his own hair was the same length, and he didn't particularly see any freedom in it. These were ways of each beginning to ask the other, "How did you get here?" but there was no neat summary in answer to that question. Here was one reason Mayfly tended to keep in touch so poorly with folks who were no longer part of her daily routine: there was always the dilemma of how to sum herself up, how to explain everywhere she'd been—and how to explain everyone she'd been—since the last point of contact.

They'd each kept moving along their separate trajectories, always intending to join back on occasion, since the night seven years ago when Ham had stood with his heels dug into the gravel of the train yard and watched Mayfly swing up onto the boxcar, watched her disappear away into the train's thin line, to join the horizon and its necklace of far-off lights.

Ham had missed her sometimes. He thought of her the following year when summer swelled up again. He thought of her sometimes when riding the streetcar on St. Charles, when air thick as cake and redolent with honeysuckle pushed through the slits in the window next to his seat. He thought of her when he saw punk kids begging in the Quarter, sometimes thought of her at the strong smell of an unwashed body.

He thought of her when he switched schools, thought of her when Father Maughn transferred parishes and was replaced by a potbellied priest from South America. Thought he saw her in a stranger sometimes, the same way he still searched every crowd for faces that looked like his own, draping the bodies of strangers with the costumes of his imagined cousins and half-siblings and great-aunts. The longing found an easy home in him.

The bus hulks into a gas station, and it heaves to a stop. They're some forty miles from Morrisville. The station's rafters, lit in blue-white fluorescence, cast an artificial day against the darkening skies. The bus passengers file out, and Ham's young seatmate doesn't seem to mind when he places his palm at the top of her head to steady himself, his senses dazed, confused that the ground beneath him no longer moves. The thirty or so strangers—not so strange to one another as they'd been a few hours ago, and with less regard for the boundaries between their bodies—shuffle their rubber soles against the rubber of the aisle. Ham files out too, feeling it in his shoulders when he jerks down to take the first step at the doorway. He can see into the window of the convenience store, where his seatmate's brother is pushing a dollar bill, worn to the texture of cloth, beneath the shield of transparent plastic that protects the cashier from the menace of the boy's burgeoning manhood, from his child's sour-milk breath.

When he'd left Morrisville, Alabama, a month ago—Alabama, where the bus now cools, Alabama, which was never his home but only a temporary refuge, where a girl named Deborah had tried her best to penetrate the numbness that had overtaken him to the soul (not knowing, as he still doesn't know, that his own child was breathing underwater like a fish in her belly, a real relative, not the imagined ones he has known)—it was because he had sought Mayfly. He had spent a strange week staying with Deborah's family after the hurricane blasted him from his hometown, moving throughout their house under the weight of the possibility that all he had ever known had been destroyed.

To escape, he had sent an email to an old address and received by chance a response. He had dialed the number she included, and when he'd heard her voice he'd come up in a car pool with others bound for various destinations in the city of Atlanta. He was dropped off a few blocks away from her place at a desolate strip mall; he'd switched two digits in her street number.

"You know," Mayfly had said as night pooled around them and the rain slowed, "I wanted to be an orphan too." She was thinking of the mud that was rising to gather around her bicycle's tires outside and what a mess she would get into trying to free them from the sludge the next day.

"Is that why you followed me home that time? To Miss Pearl's table?"

"Because we were two orphans, to my mind. I was a runaway. A fugitive. Excited by the idea that something was always on my trail, that it would catch up to me."

"No one was chasing you," Ham said.

"No," she had to agree. "That would have been more fun, right?"

"I don't know," Ham said.

"But I felt like we needed to look out for each other."

"Well," Ham said, "nobody looks out for me." It was both a boast and a lament.

They were not being chased by the same things, he wanted to say, certainly not now, and they never had been.

She said, "Don't trust me."

"What?"

"I could be here one minute, gone the next."

Ham didn't know what to make of it, but he filed it away with the other curious things.

And as they both turned inward, shaken by the dance of speaking to each other without saying anything, saying things to each other without speaking, lulled by the drone of the rain against the house's sides, they nodded to sleep, first Ham and then Mayfly.

That night on the sofa, both Ham and Mayfly had the same dream. They wandered a city at twilight, both of them children of the same age and size, until they came to the backyard of Miss Pearl's old shotgun house, a meadow of overgrown weeds and fruit. Hairy moths beat their wings against the stoop light shining like a beacon, and Ham and Mayfly were as attracted as the insects to the false moon.

Sleeping Ham and waking Ham both want to know if Miss Pearl is alive or dead. They both want to know if she has been swallowed by the raging lake that broke its bounds when the hurricane came in and spilled the contents of the ocean over the land. Sleeping Ham, much more strongly and achingly than waking Ham, would have me dredge the murky waters of the underworld for her, count every pleading face in heaven and hell and all the ones on earth. Waking Ham feels this most often as an indistinct and unnamed malaise, or sometimes like the phantom pain of a limb severed long ago.

In their shared dream the back door was wide open, and they looked on inside the bright yellow picture framed by the doorway as I set the table, placing glinting butter knives beside spoons with worn wooden handles. I wore my habit, a belt of knotted hemp rope around my waist. Steam rose in plumes from a stove just out of Ham and Mayfly's view, and the only part of Miss Pearl they could make out was the flesh of her elbow, jiggling into and out of sight as she stirred the pot.

Some hours later, nighttime was parted like a sea for Ham and Mayfly, anchored head to foot on the sofa, and the sun broke through their dreaming.

2. In which the spirit of Ham's relic makes his case

Ham is best in the sun, so let's see him there, in a memory he doesn't often recover. In it he was playing in the street with other boys, a mad game of kickball where the targets of the ball changed. He moved down the sun-warmed asphalt on feet made of feathers and flying machines, as exhilarated by the sun that illuminated the heavens as by its round counterpart on earth, a kickball that was deflated only enough to prove its worth, that it had been the object of attention. No one meant it to be a rough game but one of the other boys pushed him into the ground. He gave back as good as he got. His knee was skinned when he hit the asphalt, but he didn't complain. The wind hit his wound as he raced back down the street, but even the sting of it was a pleasure, the sun over his head pounding a heat that felt like love.

Ham had arrived at Miss Pearl's with one trash bag full of his things. They had been neatly folded by the lady at the group home: two pairs of pants, creased shorts for the summer, four T-shirts, a sweater. The plastic bag, a white one, was tied securely. Homes are places of love, he had been told by many, and in the home where he was kept with other boys there had been a bit of that, of love, from the people who were paid to watch and feed them.

Houses, on the other hand, are different things. In the house of his youngest years, he was left alone with a baby sister for days. Ham cannot recall it as I can: how Ham found potatoes in the bottom of the pantry, the only food within his small reach, washed them in toilet water, and chewed them raw, spitting some into a hand to feed to his sister, who had no teeth yet. In the house, which was more of an apartment, his mother, with shining burgundy lips, fingers ringed with gold or something like it, made her dazzling appearances alone or with some man, never the same one. Enough appearances that Ham and his sister would not die, but just barely. Back in those days—days consumed by that total whitewash, that blankness, by which memory is stored in the ligaments and in the innermost chambers of the heart where blood rushes through on its last chance at oxygenation, away from mind, away from sight—Ham loved his baby sister. She was the one shining love of his heart. Ask him her name now, see if he recalls. It would take him days to call it to mind. It's not that he never remembers her anymore, but the part of him that thinks does not. These days, postflood, he cannot have one more lost, one more among the many he's had. In order to avoid losing, you lose the thing yourself, in advance.

By the time he found himself in Miss Pearl's kitchen he'd

been taken from that house and taken from the group home. In Miss Pearl's house, the adults had their conversation, from which he was excluded, as he was shown his bedroom. They said things he wouldn't have understood about reimbursement for his foster care, which Miss Pearl hoped would bring much-needed extra money into the household. Miss Pearl made wide and sweeping gestures with her arms to show her generosity, to show that all she had carefully cultivated in this home was here for Ham's benefit. With her gracious and saintly attitude, Miss Pearl pointed out that her own son Wally had the top bunk, that Ham could take the bottom. Wally, propped up on his arms in the loft above reading a comic book, looked at Ham in wonder. That Miss Pearl considered herself a moral example above all others was not clear to Ham, and it would not have been important. He had a brother now who was not a brother, a bunk bed. A feeling that though he did not belong yet, he could work toward belonging. Ham in those days used to practice before the mirror, a doe-type look, shining black eyes that asked to be loved. If he could perfect the eyes—call a little water to them to make them shine—then he could add any facial expression. A smile maybe, but it had to be shy, showing the corner of a tooth. It got so that he could sustain the doe-look for entire conversations. He lost it at seventeen when he went out on his own, working at a fast-food restaurant; he would come home to the room he rented smelling like hot french-fry grease and chicken. The look was no longer necessary; such appearances are for boys, not men. As he had gained it by conscious will, so he lost it in favor of a glance he hoped looked hard. A glance that no one, no one, no one he has met has ever taken for hard.

Miss Pearl was one for gestures, and the doe-look was Ham's ticket to what might be termed love. She was one for gestures of propriety, decorum, and, most importantly, gratitude. And luckily enough for Ham, she was one who took the gesture for the thing itself. "You must be grateful, Ham, for all we're giving you," she told him that day. She repeated this in variation almost daily. The *we* being herself and her son, or perhaps a royal sort of *we*, for no man was to be found. Miss Pearl had given up men for a chastity she hoped would find favor in god's sight and would twist the corners of her mouth down at women she knew who had not been fortunate enough to make the same choice or have it imposed on them. The sight of a man and woman holding hands in the street was enough to induce the look. Miss Pearl's was an expression Ham would replicate sometimes in the mirror, although he never quite found the proper function for its daily use.

In a battle that had cost her any semblance of a relationship with her sister, Miss Pearl had won the family home after their mother Agnes's death. She'd hoped the house would be the epicenter of a prosperous new married life at the time but was soon heartbroken by desertion. From this heartbreak, she had fashioned a world for herself and Wally, newborn and newly fatherless, where everything had its place and everything occurred according to its time, where she could hold the reins of natural law.

Pearl had been a young child when her mother had shunted their furniture into MeeMaw Lana's old home to make it theirs. MeeMaw had been a well-heeled gris-gris queen of some local renown, but Agnes wanted none of it—she shoved the tools of her mother's trade into crevices and corners. Those trinkets and vials of colored liquid and fragments of bone were not of god and were not of upright people, according to Agnes. Pearl did not inherit all of her mother's ways, but she did learn how to wear piety as a shield against potential threats—and once she'd had a taste for the authority she could hold over others by her claims to religion, she craved it. In signaling to her neighbors and the people she met that she was a woman of faith with her frequent signs of the cross and her calculated facial expressions of disapproval, she hoped in part to deflect their attention, in part to win status. Just as with the clothes she had taken to wearing for years since she'd started to gain weight, nondescript folds in patterns meant to obscure her form, she hoped to come across as both unassuming and intimidating, and she hoped this would protect both her and her son from the savage forces that threatened on all sides.

Something wild and alien in the young boy she'd taken in threatened the careful order and authority she had enjoyed in her home, and she knew it would require tools beyond her usual arsenal. Above all else, Miss Pearl was resourceful. She wasn't above adapting one of her MeeMaw's charms to assure order was fixed in the world she ruled. It wouldn't be the first time.

The pendant with a fragment of my bone in it had belonged to Miss Pearl's MeeMaw. Despite her claims to shun gris-gris, the truth was that Pearl had absorbed a thing or two from spending time with her grandmother before she passed, lingering while MeeMaw consulted with clients, lingering while she cast her spells.

In this case, after Ham ran away for a week not long after he'd arrived, the goal was to bind. The feeling that he was something Miss Pearl and Wally bore but didn't want had gotten to him, maybe the moment he'd seen or imagined Miss Pearl wince when he went back for a second portion at dinner, as though she were calculating the exact expense he was to her, whereas Wally was free to eat as much as he wanted. So Ham escaped from Miss Pearl's house out of her bathroom window, and for that week he ate out of greasy discarded bags and begged other boys he found out filling streets with their laughter to play with him. They often relented, but at the end of the game, cops-and-robbers or whatever, shooed him away like you would a dog.

Miss Pearl considered her method. Should she beat the boy, or charm him? In light of his bedraggled appearance, and the fact that his doe-look seemed faded when he appeared on her porch again, she chose a hex. She took my relic from an old chest and handed it to Ham, who was awed by the piece. Miss Pearl needed an outlet for her boundless generosity. She was raising Wally to consider himself a person of privilege; she would raise Ham to consider himself the beneficiary of her generosity, whether he liked it or not. She knew the trinket she had given him would aid her in this, and she thanked god for it.

I began to walk up in Ham's bones the very next day, to ease his way, to help his forgetting. If he wanted to be vacant, I would fill him. When he grew into young manhood, I walked him away from Miss Pearl and into his own life. I operated him every day of his first job, dipping the fries into grease by working his arms until he could find the composure to make his own face, setting an expression into his brows that told the world not to mess with him.

The old songs of Ham's country tell of an Old Man Sorrow, who comes to rest beside you when no one else will. I have been this for many, the silent boots that come over the threshold, the creak in the old wooden chair that can only have been produced by a body. Those who pray know that our Lord Jesus Christ has a hefty waiting list and call on others like me in his stead; and if you need someone to walk you and you know the right methods, I shall. They call on me as Papa Legba in the part of the world where Ham is from, though many others will answer to that name. If the request is suitable, and the methods proper, I will come. The cost is your remembrance: if I walk through you, if I speak through you, you will recall little of it. For Ham, who learned as a teenager that sucking on sugarcane or drinking too much rum would keep me near, it's not too high a price. How much of Ham is himself anymore? It matters less than you'd think.

To the faithful it matters not that I lived. When I was living in my own body, I surrendered my life to god. They would spit at my mother, my sister, and me in the streets when I was a child, because we were poor, because my mother's color designated her as a slave and mine designated me as a bastard. My father was off to conquer another world, and there was so much of it to be conquered, so much rich tropical soil to stick a flag in, so many other human beings whose humanity needed stricter terms and conditions than the merely human. Like Ham does, I wondered if I had brothers and sisters out there in this vast new world, little mulattos and mestizos. Surrendering such impossible wonderings, I gave myself, soon as I was old enough, to true brotherhood, brotherhood in Christ, with the Dominicans.

What clothes I had I gave away. I asked to be a servant among my brothers. I beat the devil out of me nightly by every physical means. I lived in total submission to the will of one greater than I. I let this will work through me, so that I could place my hands into the wounds of the sick, leaving them healed when I withdrew. For these and other things—these things possible not because of myself but because of what, or whom, I let work through me—my body was ripped apart after death by those who had witnessed my life. This, as everyone knows, is the key to never dying, but of having eternal death. They attempted to destroy Christ's body, but in unity with his holy father he recovered something like an earthly life only three days later and slipped coolly into the heavens, wholly, only forty days after that. Imagine the havoc it would have wrought had they been able to gather his bones, partition them. As the very fabric of the universe was shifted by his sacrifice on the cross, so the fabric of earth would have ripped. We must be glad we were not witness to such a thing; the world may not have survived.

I do not profess to be our Lord and Savior. I am an infinitely humbler spirit, and this has been my fate: my bones radiating, calling to one another, calling to be made whole and returned whole to the dust from which they came. If my body cannot be found intact by the Last Day, I may risk being denied the resurrection Christ promised to share with us. So I find myself begging to be used. Often abused. And with time I have learned, fortunately or unfortunately, to lust after occupation of the human form. There are so many who call, so many who need, so many who would surrender their being to me, but for our purposes the principal of these is Ham. Who would prefer not to be himself. Who has me walking around, centuries after my birth, in his flesh. I will not, cannot, let go.

3. In which Mays past are recounted

Ham fell into the order that life in Miss Pearl's house imposed on him, a new structure that was put on his time like braces on legs. A chart where chores were posted, tasks demarcated as either Ham's or Wally's, was stuck to the refrigerator with alphabet magnets. Sheets and blankets to be tucked so tight when beds were made in the morning that a butter knife had trouble wedging between them, and Miss Pearl would apply the butter-knife test herself, even climbing a ladder to the top bunk, at least twice weekly. No dessert with dinner except on Sundays, when after church Miss Pearl roasted a chicken, still wearing her high-heeled shoes as she cooked.

School at Our Lady of Prompt Succor was where you sat as one of a neatly organized mass, behind a girl, Claudie, with ribbons braided into her hair, and where your voice joined a chorus of other kids when the priest entered the room on his morning tour. "Good morning, boys and girls," Father Maughn would say, the singsong chorus of "Good morning, Father Maughn" echoing in return. And where you didn't tell if he left his hand too long over yours if you were called to him alone. Others, it was said, had suffered worse fates than to drown in Father Maughn's swampy breath a few minutes too long.

For the first half of the school year, Wally didn't say a word to Ham at school. They were strangers there. On Wally's sub-conscious cue, Ham averted his eyes when they passed in the hallway. Wally would sit several rows ahead of him on the school bus, would make sure to gather enough exuberance to beat Ham to the front door by at least a few minutes. Once inside Miss Pearl's house, though, things changed. A fraternal punch in the shoulder, a race from the front to the back of the house.

Ham had to earn the right to be acknowledged at school. The opportunity came when he found a dead sparrow at recess once, cupped it into his hands, and held the breast that wasn't beating to his ear, as though the heart's ghost might make some sound. "Whatcha gonna do with it?" shouted someone from the curious crowd, mostly girls, that circled around him. Let it go, Ham was going to tell them, but someone had the idea to put it on a teacher's chair. So five minutes before class started, he did it, head numb with the pounding of his heart, so dizzy he felt he might be sick as he took his place back in his seat. On cue in the production he had staged, Mrs. Glover sat in her chair.

On cue, shrieks and squeals through hands clasped over mouths as the classroom erupted. To this day it's the closest Ham has come to a feeling of applause, and his dizziness cast a gauze over everything, made it a haze. The aftereffects were subtle; he did not become any kind of god, did not become central to the social function of their school in any way. But Wally said, "What's up?" the next day in the hallway. He had become someone you could say "What's up?" to.

That was a time when Ham was his own, before I'd been allowed to enter. The day he put the dead sparrow on Mrs. Glover's chair, his head spun. But he stood up as himself. Patted his body to make sure it was all there. Got a drink of water when he could and the dizziness went away.

He knows that he crowned the statue of Mary with the other kids at school that May, knows that the wind shook the trees in the grotto until they rained tiny snow-like blossoms over everyone, that the high sun was a warmth on their foreheads, imprinting itself there. That even the stone Virgin was warm to the touch when Ham, restless, put a palm to her foot, under which a stone snake writhed in defeat.

What of Miss Pearl's Mays? Which Mays had made her who she was? Ham wonders whether she's alive or dead now, whether her house still stands or leans cockeyed underwater. See: Miss Pearl, then a young girl wedged between her sister and a cousin on the sticky back seat of a Chevrolet twisting down the small road beside the water, craning her neck to watch it out of the window—

watch how water could vanish like that, meet sky and break free of itself. As though the clouds had summoned the water to change form: claim your inheritance, become one of us, drift above the waters of the whole world.

Her grandmother MeeMaw, the gris-gris queen, took them out to gather mayhaws late every spring, when the berries were expected to be full and dark. She shuffled whoever was around into the car, a polished, pampered, bright red thing she had bought with her own money and tended and guarded as well as some people did their animals. They drove an hour and a half out while the city thawed into country and the lampposts that arched over their path transformed into trees that stooped above the road to touch the fingers of their friends across the way.

Compare the life span of one of these trees to the life span of MeeMaw. In the moment it took for one of these trees to strain tip-toed above the others who competed for their bit of sun, in the moment it took for that tree to be overtaken again by a neighbor, Miss Pearl's MeeMaw had been born and lived all the previous years of her life. While the tree raised high a piece of wire someone had twisted into it, while this wire rusted and then crumbled, MeeMaw had herself been raised and had come of age. She had learned to conjure from the Indian woman whose daughter she'd saved from drowning. Had helped into and out of binds the customers of every color who came begging her for health, money, revenge, or the love of the unwilling. In this time she had also borne a child each to three different wealthy men, two white and one colored, none of whom she would have married even if she could have. She had watched at least one daughter, Pearl's mother Agnes, grow up to become embarrassed of her and marry into piety, and later welcomed this daughter and the others onto her porch, regardless of the past, with children of their own.

MeeMaw's gloved hands steered them all farther and farther from civilization—a word Pearl had learned was for tall buildings, good manners, and the way white people's lips shaped their vowels—and the roads became gravel, then dirt, then mud. Then MeeMaw jolted them off the road, where they parked. In the air, pollen shimmered like golden dust and thousands of insects churned their tiny motors. This day, the girls, Pearl and her cousins, each swinging baskets half their size beside them, trailed behind MeeMaw like ducklings, the mud sucking at their boots. MeeMaw always chose a good stick that she would swing before them like a machete, parting the growth for them to stomp on through.

She liked to bring the little ones with her so she could have someone climb the tree and shake the small red jewels, ripe to bursting, from its branches. She favored one specific tree and had returned to it every year since she herself was a child, finding her way to it by how it smelled, by the slant of the sunlight that shifted as they approached in a way only she could detect, because the wind through its leaves rang a very particular chord. When she met the tree she removed her gloves, and she put her hand to its trunk in greeting, feeling the sap pulsing within it,

then took an old tablecloth from her bag and spread it on the
ground. Pearl was not a sure enough climber to keep her bal-
ance while avoiding the tree's thorns, so it was her sister Pauline
who shimmied up easily as a baby squirrel, cousin Lucille not
far behind her. Pearl was jealous of the sighing of the rustling
leaves and the laughter of the older girls in the boughs, everything of them hidden but the flicker of a yellow shirt, the flash
of a blue dress, but she was assuaged the minute she took up a
fruit that had fallen and its sweet, forgiving juice flooded her
mouth. MeeMaw's part in the process was to stand ankle-deep
on the other side of the tree's shadow where the mud of the
swamp became muddy water, plucking fallen mayhaws from
where they floated. Pearl had held her breath to watch a water moccasin's metallic scales glint beneath the shallow water as
it curved to approach her grandmother, curious, but MeeMaw
only stared the snake in its yellow eyes, as though she were the
one whose venom should be feared.

This was the image that came to Miss Pearl's mind when
she met the dirty girl Ham dragged with him, many summers
later, into her MeeMaw's very home, now hers. The girl's smell
preceded her. May-something-or-other, and Pearl remembered
for the first time in a long while looking at her grandmother
from the back, the knobs of the older woman's straight spine
outlined when the breeze rippled her blouse, her feet submerged
and her skirt tied up, her head tied up too, in cloth, and tilted
perhaps because she was breathing in the springtime and savor-
ing a moment that only came once a year, but every year, like a
birthday.

"What you say her name is? Mayhaw?" Miss Pearl whispered to Ham when the girl was gone to the bathroom.

"—fly," Ham said.

"Strange." But Pearl threw three more crabs in the pot.

4. In which Ham is enraptured by the dream of Mayfly

Miss Pearl saw signs and wonders in the world. Her life was ordered by herself, the world by god, who would punish her enemies and damn wrongdoers to hell, assuredly. A cloud passing overhead with a certain speed told her something she didn't even need to tell herself. But she had not forecast Mayfly or how she would change Ham. It was evidenced by a sleeplessness, a near-constant wandering off of his attention, a seeming refusal to be here now. Vacancies I took hold of. Miss Pearl saw it as a change in Ham, whom she at times likened in her mind to an animal whose spirit needed breaking.

They had met at the corner store, where Ham was sent to buy milk. In line behind him, Mayfly kicked his calves, and he turned and she laughed at him. He laughed back. She asked him where he was headed to. She stood a head or so above him, her hair a lion's mane, a garden, dreadlocks tumbling into and out of one another and falling like the fringe on her skirt. "Home," he said, and she followed him there, where she ate crabs with Ham, Miss Pearl, and Wally.

He was after her like a blind follower for the month or so she stayed in town that summer, a time when the hot, thick air took form and applied a choke hold to your senses. He went anywhere she led, into abandoned warehouses, with their industrial windows of broken glass, cobwebs, creaky floors, and into secret gardens where fruits and vegetables grew. They weren't friends; Mayfly could never be friends with someone eight years younger than her worldly nineteen, was barely a friend to the friends she had. But she let him be her shadow. He ran errands for her. He showed her what he knew of alleyways you could take to get somewhere faster.

Mayfly was the child of immigrants to the upper middle class, the child of two headstrong college graduates, the first in their families, who had determined to take their slice of the national dream as soon as history made it available to them. She was the granddaughter of women who had labored in the homes of the wealthy and the descendant many times over of men who had tilled the property of the wealthy and peopled their factories, working always in rows, filing home after dark to ply their livers with harsh homemade liquor on one another's porches.

Mayfly was a migrant, the daughter of itinerant professionals, transferred here and there across the country in allegiance to the corporations that employed them. When she left their home after high school she never looked back. She and her folks didn't see eye to eye on anything. When her mother had discovered she hadn't applied to any colleges as she'd said she had and screamed "Doesn't the future mean anything to you?" at her in the dining room, vibrating the nice china, it was all the signal Mayfly had needed to free herself of their expectations, and she fled their home that night. She was welcomed onto the porch of a farmhouse one county over, occupied by white kids with matted hair, nests of it, and with worn T-shirts and musical instruments tinkered at with varying degrees of skill and commitment. They saved the scraps of every meal, the crumbling shells of every egg, the peelings of all vegetables, and put them into a can in the corner that was separate from the trash. When the mass began to soften with rot, they took it to spread as fertilizer on the vast garden outside. She learned to love kneeling in the sun beside someone who had become a friend, coaxing new forms from the black earth.

There no one asked her, as had her classmates at the new school she moved to in fifth grade, whether her skin got darker in the sun like theirs did, and if so how. No one told her, as had her classmates the following year when the school musical was cast, that she looked like she could sing, not even in the evenings when a guitar would come out and a drum was passed around.

How easy it was for her to sit with Ham and Miss Pearl when she found them a year or so later, in the city she'd wandered to with a friend and a friend's friend on their long summer trip across the country on freight trains. The long summer trip, their birthright, had been suggested to them too earnestly and compellingly by the past few generations of books and blues songs to resist. How easy to start a conversation with the little boy ahead of her in line at a corner store clutching the carton of milk he'd been sent to buy so tightly his knuckles paled. How easy to follow him across the city, to have her fortune read with his in the square in front of an old church, and to take the seat beside him at Miss Pearl's table that evening and suck the meat out of steaming crab legs, she and Ham and Miss Pearl and Wally throwing what remained into one pile on a bed of newspaper in the table's center. How easy to slip in somewhere she might have a place, and how easy to leave.

She wallowed in the grime of that city for about a month and a half. The friends who had traveled with her were Nora and Christopher, the three sometimes joined by Christopher's drag alter ego Adelaide. There were a few houses in the city where they were warmly welcome. In Mayfly's time in the city that summer she would drift freely between these and Miss Pearl's house. The first night the three had arrived together, lungs choked by the rich air off the bayous surrounding the city, they stayed with Adelaide's ex-bandmate. Mayfly and Nora shared an air mattress in the kitchen, on their backs, respecting an invisible line down the mattress's middle, staring up into the blackness where they imagined a ceiling, a cap on the formless black that might have spooled upward forever. The night began to storm, suddenly and wildly, around 2:00 a.m. Rain and hail tore at the windows and clawed at the ground, and they heard the trees thrashing in agony, bending so low as to graze the earth, heard the shrubs lashing like whips. Hurricane, Mayfly had thought sleepily, this the most accurate word her unthawed mind could pull from its darkness.

That was all long ago. The home of Mayfly's friends, where she'd been staying when she met Ham, had been erased by the floods. Long before the building was washed away, the occupants Ham had known had gathered themselves, stripped its walls, and left. Mayfly had moved on too. But he wants to think of that house as hers. The house stays fixed in his mind, stronger than memory: somewhere he is going to trace his way back to, sometime. It has a place of high honor on his old map, that map of his city back when it was his whole world, with its layers of the past peeking out from beneath everything everywhere, unfurling without warning into any present moment. He would work as hard as he could to earn his way back to that place. The child in him, with child logic, convinced him that his recent ordeals were a kind of penance— that now the storm has humbled him, something greater waits for him. For god so loves those who suffer.

To know how real this dream is for him, imagine boy-Ham led by the hand of a younger Mayfly to a front yard about seven blocks from Miss Pearl's house. It was morning, and Ham and Mayfly ate a breakfast of yesterday's biscuits from Miss Pearl's refrigerator. Ham finicked with his food, pressing his finger into the center of each biscuit half, where the cold butter had gelled. They washed them down with glasses of milk, rinsed sleep from their faces with water from the kitchen sink, and went out into the day. Their cheeks, still wet, would have stung at first encounter with the morning's cool.

Sheltered by the leathery leaves of the magnolia tree that arched over the chain-link fence, they stopped at the iron gate of Adelaide's ex-bandmate Todd's house, where four young people lived officially and three—Mayfly, Nora, Adelaide—were welcome transients for now. Mayfly slid her hand through the gap between the gate and the fence, unhitching the lock from behind so that the gate swung wide. Ham saw a garden, an oasis, a paradise thick with shade.

There, the sun glinted off the metal of bicycle parts and other twisted, shining odds and ends: a rake and shovel, an antique television with a shattered screen. He saw a tall live oak tree from whose sturdy branches a rope swing hung. There was a chicken coop from which a proud bald turkey made an exit, strutting out to stare defiantly at Ham from behind a wire mesh enclosure— lord of the fowl, he took his place among the white chickens and dark roosters that scattered to give him wide enough berth. Mayfly led Ham under trees dripping mangoes and others whose branches were low with bananas, along a gravel path that led up to the front porch.

A white boy with long limbs sat in a rocking chair on the porch rolling himself a cigarette. Ham studied the quick motion of his fingers, how they transformed the raw materials before them into something sleek, solid, and tightly packed. Able to be tucked, as Christopher did now, behind an ear. Mayfly greeted him. In monotone he said, "What's up," and then asked, "Who's this?"

"Oh, this is Ham," Mayfly had said. Ham mumbled what he hoped passed for words of greeting, and he and Mayfly trudged inside, to a lost world where found objects were arranged discordantly. The broad yellow diamond of a stolen traffic sign glowed with reflective paint in the corner. Three or four stopped clocks hung in a row on one wall. Chairs were missing seats, backs, cushions; the paisley upholstery upon the couch had been sullied and dulled by decades. In a makeshift library with shelves made from cinder blocks and unfinished wooden boards, a 1913 German encyclopedia kept company with hundreds of moldy paperbacks. There was a kitchen, the sink piled high with dishes.

Mayfly had asked him if he'd like some coffee. "We just dumpstered it yesterday morning. Good stuff, Brazilian, from some yuppie café on Magazine."

It was a grown-up request; no one had ever offered Ham coffee in his eleven years. The gesture, and Ham's acceptance of it, gave him something to do with himself besides play with his hands, out of place, waiting to be spoken to. It gave him a posture to try on, a persona to slip into. He would be a coffee drinker here, a man of the world, someone who knew exactly what the deal was, and he would carry himself as such. This Ham, for whom a cup of coffee was as routine and natural as anything, was one bold enough to ask questions—not ones like "What's yuppie mean?" that intimated how much he didn't know, but ones to which he already assumed an answer, like "This where you live?" And when the answer he assumed was wrong, he didn't let on.

"No, no. I'm not from here, I thought I told you. Todd lives here."

"The one on the porch?"

"That's Christopher. We're traveling together."

"From where?"

Mayfly shrugged. "Everywhere."

Ham could not explain the thrill he experienced there among these broken things, these odd things and their scents. His nose sent him rotting fruit, bodies rich with ripe funk, and somewhere

the fresh chemical smell of wet paint. He took in his surround-
ings in silence, bringing the coffee to his lips and not complain-
ing when it burned, instead lowering it patiently and coolly. A
wooden ladder led from the first floor to the one above it, where
the voices of two or three people were muffled in conversation
and their heavy steps rattled the light bulb on the kitchen ceiling.
This was a lost, secret world. It was musky and sweet like sweat,
and it was dirty like the woods were dirty; decay had a natural
place here.

He had never been among people who lived like this. The
dirt of houses where he had been was sometimes accidental, occasionally even neglectful, but most often it was eliminated at its
very beginnings with zeal, cleanliness being, if not next to god,
if not next to wealth, at least next to pride in what one did own.
That was the way Ham saw cleanliness too, had from a young age
and always would. But being here among Mayfly's clan, in her
territory—seeing that she was not an exception to the order of
things but had a place among others like her—did something to
his senses, inflated things out of proportion so that he did indeed
feel very small, even smaller than he actually was, perched on a
wobbly chair with his feet too high to touch the ground. It was all
he could do to grip the hot cup in his hands, claim it, and allow
it to confer some of its privilege on him. No sugar to dilute its
strength, no cream to cloud its depths; in it he saw the very color
and liquid quality of his own eyes.

"I just love me some coffee," he said with authority. Mayfly
laughed. "It's good," she agreed. "The kids upstairs," she let him

know, "are painting the walls. They started yesterday." A deep midnight color, a blue so black—I see it for Ham.

He was sure this was what he had always been looking for, and since then he's looked for it everywhere. No other place has captured him the same way. It was like a hidden part of the world, where time moved differently and he felt he occupied a different self. He could not explain why, out of all the houses he had been in, it was this one, this one that still stands alone for him. Something was born in him there.

5. In which fortunes are told and lots are cast

The bodies of the people of Belen who greeted Columbus were dripping with gold. This much has been remembered, has been recorded. Golden orbs dropped tear-like from the ears of their women, so that everyone glowed with the sun and twinkled when the breezes flicked the sudden glint of daylight off the edge of a charm. Years later my own mother wore a brass hawk's bell around her neck, which was rumored to have been given to the people of Belen by Columbus himself. She had heard from the old man who'd given it to her when she was a girl of how the very figure of Columbus had blocked out the sun to the people who stood to meet him, so that a halo of stolen light encircled him.

Such a pretty little bell for a pretty little girl.

When my father was a boy and heard that a paradise was discovered in the Far East, where birds of every color were blown about by spice-scented breezes, a seed was planted in him. As soon as he could pry himself out of his family's embrace, he promised a minor nobleman five years of labor in the New World in return for a small hammock webbed across a dusty corner in the belly of the next ship out of Seville.

There was enough in the Indies for the taking. Any fool could crown himself king of whatever he himself uncovered.

My father, then a skinny man-child who couldn't yet grow a full beard, found himself clambering up onto the deck the day land was sighted. The sea in this part of the world was the bluest kind of blue, a bright screen over an underwater world where brilliantly colored fish flicked between patches of coral. Up ahead, plumes of smoke rose above the thick forests onshore. The smoke issued from the signal fires the Indians lit to warn neighboring villages that the foreigners' ships had been spotted. On disembarking he found himself in Panama, wide-eyed at the newness of the world.

I can remember my father pulling me onto his knee. I can't make out the features of his face anymore; they are as far away as the sky. I remember the shelflike chin, my head nestled underneath it. Most of all I remember the great expanse of his torso, a grand and solid hill. I remember the arms forested in hair and his thick pale hands. By then he was a lord, master of all he surveyed. I remember wriggling in his rough grip—a soldier's awkward grasp, better suited for holding weapons.

My mother said I had his brow. She said I had a way of screwing up my face in concentration that was just like him.

To my mother's mind, my body and my sister's body could be

broken into atomic components that favored different ancestors, which bode well or ill of things to come for us. She told my sister, Juana, that she always knew she would take up wool-dyeing one day, because Juana had a dimple in her chin as did our great-great-aunt in Dahomey who was known to have spun beautiful, wide tapestries.

In the last year of my life on earth my sister wove me a robe of alpaca, dyed in rich carmine. She had begun to raise little cochineal bugs on the plants in her yard to crush into brilliant red dye herself. My vows required me to reject this gift of hers, though it was a magnificent piece of work. Although she knew that I would never take it home, I believe that Juana would deliberately hang it above the door on days when I came to see her, so that she could imagine I had just removed it myself and set it there upon entering. This robe belonged not to me but to Juana's imaginary brother, someone with my dimensions who wore fine things out into the world, who turned the eyes of passersby toward the splendor of his crimson robe as he swished down the avenue.

But I let the details of that life slip from me. I suppose in the long years since, I have become Juana's imaginary brother again, that wanderer far past the bounds of the body, my recollection as scattered as the parts of my body that my Dominican brothers nicked from me in the morgue—the end joint of a finger, a lock of hair here, a tooth.

The body is the first homeland. When it is destroyed, we are set to everlasting exile. Until, like some parasite, we can find a temporary home in someone else's living sinews.

It is what I have been fated to do: fill vacancies the living have left within themselves, seize them, and love them. They call me, though they don't all realize it. Some do. But others are calling simply, blindly, for love. As Ham did when he was a child (weak as children are weak and open as children are open), holding within his small fist the charm he would wear around his neck from that time forward: that minor fleck of my shattered body.

He wore the relic around his neck when he visited a fortune-teller in the square in his hometown with Mayfly, the day they first met. It was me who moved the fortune-teller's hands that day. She'd been exhausted after a night of tossing sleeplessly on her bedbug-ridden mattress in between tending to her daughter's stomach sickness, propping the half-asleep child between her own knees in the bathtub at 1:00 a.m. to rinse the vomit out of the girl's hair. Through the cracks in the fortune-teller's tired mind that morning, I entered. It was me, then, looking out from her head at those first two pitiful customers of the day, a young girl and younger boy, would-be ruffians.

The fortune-teller, Lily, wasn't immune to the odd crisis of faith. Some days, sucking on a Pall Mall with her legs crossed on that park bench, she didn't believe there was a future at all, just now, and now all over again the next day. Or else she couldn't bring herself to believe we were only dolls jerked about by bigger forces, sure that any sudden move on our parts could rip fate's web. She sometimes suspected that not even the planets were really locked into their orbits, that they could all fly loose and go hurtling everywhere at once. Or that on some days, everything literally disappears when you close your eyes for that split second before you open them again.

But she was determined to live, at least until something better came along, off of the fantasies and desires of tourists who washed up in town—pilgrims, really, in search of good times with the zeal of fanatics, looking to be baptized in liquor, yearning for the bottomless void of the sublime.

They wanted to be saved, each and every one. And what was she but the idol at which they laid their hopes? So what more could she do then but listen to their pleas?

"I see a fork in your path," she'd told the girl. "The one road is you among others, but you take the other."

"And you," she'd told Ham, the young boy who gazed in rapt attention. "You'll live past the end of the world."

It proved true.

6. In which the virtues of solitude are considered

Mayfly's arrival in Ham's life coincided with mine. He was given the trinket with my relic in it not three weeks before they met. What to make of the confluence, two influences now mixing in Ham like warmer and cooler streams? Was Mayfly a force to pull Ham in the opposite direction, to test Miss Pearl's ability to bind him with the relic? Someone who came into his life to urge him toward the unpredictable, the unruly, or the disordered? Was she a foil? Or was Mayfly none of those, just a lost soul like Ham who hadn't found her anchor yet in the way Miss Pearl so desperately hoped Ham was beginning to?

Mayfly's life, of course, went on far past her summer with Ham. Once, when she and Nora were traveling to Santa Fe together, Mayfly became separated from her friend. She hadn't meant to, had assumed Nora was behind her, to realize a hundred miles on as the rising sun began to alight (red, dry, and alien as the planet Mars) that her only companions in the boxcar were a father-son pair of bums, harmless men with matching beards who kept themselves dulled to near-but-not-quite sleep by means of a jug of brandy passed between them. They offered Mayfly some, and she took one small sacramental swig, to show she meant no harm, but left the rest to them, wanting to be alert, to hold her limbs flexed and to trace every sound in her hearing: the great lonely wail of the train—which traveled across the vast and rocky desert unmet by its echo—and the sounds of what she badly wanted to imagine as forlorn coyotes but might just as well have been penned-up backyard dogs, away in suburbs whose only ru-mor of anything wild in the world was the occasional train heard to holler in the distance (she could know herself, at least, as a part of this distance).

When she'd arrived in Santa Fe and Nora did not appear, did not sulk down off a car on the opposite end of the train, she could not wait by the tracks forever. She went into the town to find out where all the punk kids stayed and by nightfall was of-fered a hammock at a house where three boys lived with five cats. Bone-tired, rocked by the hammock, falling in and out of the darkest sleep, she waited two days until the shallow wave of ar-riving and departing kids—to whom, if she was awake, she would wave, nod, or engage in a few syllables, regal from her swinging perch—brought news that a traveler had arrived, a redheaded girl who was looking for Mayfly.

And so she found Nora hunched over a plate of quinoa at a local co-op not far from the boys' house. She pulled a chair across from her so that Nora could tell her, as she had surely practiced several times every day they'd been separated, "Thanks for leaving me."

"I thought you were right behind me," Mayfly said, folding her hands together and resting them on the table like she was in prayer or conducting business. "Honest. I thought you wanted some space. I thought maybe you were mad at me."

"Well, I wasn't then," Nora said. It had always been hard to read her moods, perhaps because, like Mayfly herself and like most people either of them knew at the time, she carried a sort of general anger about her, looked at all times armed and ready to cut ties. Nora said, "You didn't care what happened to me."

"That's not true."

Nora tried again: "You have no idea what happened to me."

Mayfly thought, as Nora intended her to think, You say *what* but mean *which*—of the horrors a girl traveling alone could endure without bearing much of a scar. A journey alone could be fatal.

At the time they were traveling, Mayfly lived with Nora and about twelve others in an old warehouse in Queens. They had transformed the building into a kind of rotting palace, with chambers and antechambers one after the other. In one of the rooms was a ping-pong table they had salvaged from a heap of cast-off things found on the sidewalk. Another room was filled from wall to wall with reassembled computers and parts of computers. On the roof they kept a goat and grew many of the vegetables they ate in a sprawling potted garden that Mayfly tended. They ate around a table they had built with their own hands from pine and sealed with pitch, big enough to seat twelve or fifteen, in a high-ceilinged makeshift kitchen where wonders of vegan cuisine were produced using two hot plates and an electric frying pan. But Mayfly came to feel unwelcome there, nudged from its edges. Something long, deep, and wide had grown between her and Nora after the two made their way home from Santa Fe; they avoided being in the same room together. If one entered, the other, seeing her, left. Mayfly felt the same deep, unbridgeable thing creep between her and each of the others in the house. It was only a matter of time before she would leave.

When she did finally make the journey down to Atlanta, alone, it was as someone who had hurled herself across every possible distance, bisected the country in an electric line again and back many times.

What hadn't she seen, at that point? She had seen the moon roll across low-country hills to fix itself in the sky. She had seen the sun poke a hole with each of its fingers through the brush cover of forests in Oregon. She had seen the Great Lakes, vast unforgiving water indifferent to itself. She had run beside rivers on the tracks of many a train.

She had traveled from darkness into blinding brightness and into the unique mysteries of many days from the safe warmth of the ones before them, warm at least in memory. She had traveled from summer into winter—as when she rode upward from the southernmost tip of Florida (with its palm trees splayed like drunken revelers across its beaches) until she arrived two days later in Pennsylvania, where snow sat atop the Alleghenies, eternal and unreachable, which gave her pause to marvel at the water, the ice and powder of it looking like it had never known anything else. She wondered if the snow had been raised on tales of the exploits of a pantheon of running-water gods and if it expected to become clouds when it died.

Mayfly was always on the run, like water. Whether she'd been born on the run or was set to running by circumstance was hard to say. There was no lack of material comfort in her childhood. Two good-enough parents had poured themselves into being able to communicate affection through the kind of lifestyle they could provide their daughter, music lessons and the vacations where the family of three would occupy a suite in a hotel at the mountains or the beach, the parents' bedroom adjoining hers and the door between those two rooms left open so that for a week in the summer there was no letting down the rigid mask of cordiality the members of the household maintained with one another. Perhaps each of the three of them was an outsider in this strange triad, bound by bonds of heredity and marriage. But her parents never seemed to be acting when they sat up very straight at the tables in country club and hotel dining rooms and shared their intelligence on what the neighbors were up to with one another. Or at least they fooled her and led her to believe she was the odd one out, a feeling that follows her, a circumstance she imposes on social dynamics that threaten to include her. She had been raised in a series of gated communities across the country. The last was in Virginia, in a town whose pretty squares were filled with marigolds, with benches for retirees to sit feeding seagulls and pigeons, whose avenues hosted a steady stream of cars of modern makes and models. In Virginia, her parents' white neighbors didn't bother not to stare at them, the only family of color in town. Whether she was born or made a rambler, the feeling was deep in her that she would belong nowhere, that there was nowhere for her, and she'd best get moving along if ever there appeared to be. Better do it first than get shut out and bear the sting.

She was a veteran of the road, then, when she stumbled south to Atlanta, where Ham found her next, many years later. She could read the wind at least as well as a sailor could. She knew when the air carried trouble or mercy. And knew how to draw solitude to herself and be comforted by it.

Ham, as a boy, never looked for solitude. It chased him, and he mostly managed to outrun it. While things lasted at Miss Pearl's, he felt he had a real brother in Wally. Wally became his passcode to places he would otherwise be denied. Wally was Ham's don't-worry-he's-with-me, the sign to others that Ham was passable. It worked in their middle school, and it worked in high school, earning Ham the spot next to the driver of a car packed with teenage boys, one of whose older brothers had bought them all rum. One time because of Wally a girl let him kiss her, a furtive fumbling of mouths behind the bleachers while tree frogs screeched.

I walked him through his days at high school sometimes. He was overwhelmed by things others would take in stride, like the flood of people that filled the hallways between classes, like the strangely feudal social order. Once he discovered alcohol— tentatively—it became easier for me to access him. The devotee drinks away parts of himself that I can fill. It is not hard to jerk around a booze-drenched limb, to make a wine-stained mouth speak. Liquor makes the body an open door; anyone can walk in.

I often did. I'd do whatever I wanted in Ham's body after he was good and loose. I'd sometimes make his legs run, run for the sake of operating a pair of legs and feeling a breeze against flesh, and leave him to deal with the exhaustion later.

7. In which all is washed clean

Why not remember that before my spirit rose from it, before it was ripped to shreds, forever denying it the resurrection of the End of Days, my body came once, late in the fall, down the pebble-paved road to my sister's house? That I carried a dog in my arms whose muzzle was stuck with porcupine quills? And that the garlands of jasmine that curled against the stucco walls of Juana's house sent their perfume out ahead to greet me? Now that scent and touch are no longer mine, I am left with memory. Jerked here and there by the cries of the faithful, knowing what their bodies know only in translation.

And when I entered, I set the animal down, found a place at the table—accepted a bowl of soup and bread and water, accepted a child on my knee as Juana mock-chided me, "Another patient for the hospital, Martin?" sucking her teeth before this gesture could run away with itself, before her puckered lips could find themselves tugged into the thinnest smile. But together Juana and I took the animal to the pen out back with the others—the cat with the broken leg, the llama with a cold—and after my lunch I'd set out to tend to it, and for this Juana liked to call me the saint of mice, teasing.

After our mother died, my four years of seniority no longer seemed to have any bearing on Juana. In her home I was not a friar but a bachelor, someone with no household of his own, free from adult cares and responsibilities. I was a child who had yet to pass to the next stage of life. And after I'd become head of the monastery, I took some comfort in playing that role on my visits to her home: a place where my powers as a healer were neither taxed nor in demand, not appreciated but tolerated as the irksome habit of a loved one. Someone like me is most comfortable where he is uncomfortable. Juana loved me and knew this—that I needed to play her naughty child. Her briskness with me was her kindness, and for my sake she put a rough edge to her voice. She was kinder than the whip I still applied to myself, alone in my spare quarters, some nights, and she knew that too.

Like my sister, Miss Pearl kept her garden well. Nothing edible grew in it by her hand, though certain hollow blades of grass near the picket fence, when pulled from the ground, revealed themselves to young explorers like Ham and Wally to be the tops of wild spring onions, bulbs that had planted themselves there in defiance of human cultivation and which Ham and Wally and their friends in the neighborhood chopped up with sharp sticks on occasion, to use as an ingredient in pretend food that they pretend cooked for one another on the hot asphalt out front.

There were three neat, concentric rings of violets encircling each of the yard's four large trees. There were tires, painted bright white, stacked pleasingly on top of one another. One tire, placed in the garden's center, also painted white, had been slit many times at the top so parts of it spilled out in an even fringe. In the center of this was a pot that held a flowering indigo plant. The trees each had a white-painted ring around their trunks, and from one of them hollow bottles of every color were hung with string. The wind would whistle through these bottles, as if making for itself an absentminded tune, or it would clink them softly together like chimes; the sun bled their blues and greens and reds and molasses browns onto the grass below. A pebble pathway, lined on its sides by brick, led from one tree to another, and the garden's two wooden benches had also been painted white.

Still remaining from a time when the house had belonged to Miss Pearl's grandmother was a fading mural that ran along the back fence: coal-black faceless figures wearing bright clothes had been frozen in the middle of an exuberant dance by the artist— one of MeeMaw's clients, who, with little money to give MeeMaw for her miraculous return of the runaway dog he had despaired of ever seeing again to his doorstep with something newly docile in its wet black eyes, had arranged to use his talents as a painter to beautify her fence as payment. He did so, stopping only twice to wipe the sweat that poured from his brow, in full sun across three blindingly hot days one July in the middle of the last century. There was a cat painted in the lower left corner, its eye on the painted mouse that skittered to dodge the perilous footfall of the dancers toward the center of the mural.

It was the kind of picture that children like Ham imagined coming alive, the figures unsticking themselves from their two-dimensional poses on the wood to dance under the sun. Or else he imagined himself with them, imagined that one of the slender faceless women or men plucked him from out of the world and took him in their arms and whisked him across their dance floor. Ham had sat under the bottle tree in solitude many afternoons, cast with its colors, drifting somewhere until he was called for dinner. The yard was a place of peace, everything in it still.

Miss Pearl's MeeMaw would have clucked her tongue or even laughed to know that nothing that could sustain a life came out of the dirt of her garden as it was tended by her granddaughter. She would have been puzzled that Pearl kept a garden entirely for its beauty—no carrots tunneled underground, waving their green tops between the tire sculpture and the bottle tree, as they had tunneled below and waved between an attractively rusted figure wrought out of an old rake and the same tree, bearing strings of beads rather than bottles, when Pearl was a child and the yard was her grandmother's. This entirely ornamental garden was not in the front of the house, where it could be appreciated by the community, but in the back, where only the bold or the invited came. MeeMaw's practical view had been that people need both beauty and food to sustain themselves and that these could and should exist happily alongside each other in one's yard. But these were days when fewer understood that vegetables came out of black soil, that meat did not descend, shrink-wrapped manna, from the heavens.

In the version she took to her grave, or hasn't yet, depending on which story you choose to believe, Miss Pearl handed the locket with a shard of my bone in it to Ham after cradling him in her arms and singing him a lullaby, ignoring that even at a small eleven years old his limbs spilled over her lap. He did not consider losing the necklace or accidentally giving it away; something gripped him, the curiosity of it grew into a kind of comfort.

Ham doesn't care if her love was secondhand or whether she considered it charity. It wasn't that these considerations had never occurred to him, but he had little use for them. How could he compare the love she felt for Wally, her flesh and blood, with the love she felt for him? He had never asked her whether she loved him. He sees it as a stupid question. Whatever's there, you feel it. Whatever's not there, you imagine it. Ham is a big fan of certain kinds of one-sided relationships, relationships that find their color from his imagining emotions in the other that may or may not actually appear. Such relationships have never failed him yet; they are designed against failure.

These are the loves Ham holds to himself, thinking also, for the strangest of reasons, of a girl who was now waiting for him in Alabama. Was Miss Pearl's shotgun house, its bright blue coat of paint kept fresh by an unemployed alcoholic man in the neighborhood who did odd jobs for cash, really the oasis Ham wants it to be? For Miss Pearl it was another example of the reliability of the universe, a home she had known as a child, that her child now came to know. It was an homage to her grandmother and to herself, the place where she housed all her trinkets of respectability, like the doilies she would put on the coffee table if a guest of stature came through, as few did, and the family photographs and the glass figurines and the pewter rosary coiled like candies in a dish in the salon. For Wally it was a given, something he took for granted as surely as the sun shone, a place of rest and welcome where he was treasured, another prize to show to visitors. For Ham it was everything, somewhere he could belong to even if the belonging went better with physical distance. He left willingly. He didn't want to be any trouble anymore, and he didn't want Miss Pearl trotting her Sunday-best smile out to answer him when he called while her eyes belied something else—resentment or indifference.

Miss Pearl had been cut to part-time at the real estate agency where she was a secretary and things were tight. The air was taut; he could sense the change in the way Miss Pearl was doling out portions at mealtime, the way her hand stopped over Wally's plate, wanting to give him more, but dipped back into the pot she was serving from anyway, dutifully serving Ham. Of his own accord, Ham left. He was seventeen, big enough to fend for himself. He remembers standing in Miss Pearl's parlor feeling like he was getting shipped off to a war of some kind with his things and the thanks-for-everything speech he'd been mentally preparing all morning. He didn't know whether it was the kind of goodbye where you hoped to see the person soon, or later, or at all. Miss Pearl smelling of soap when they hugged and his nose graced her neck, and he wasn't sure if this was a moment where you were supposed to cry or want to.

The house had grown into him, so it became something he could call his, an extension of his very form. He liked how he knew which floorboard to avoid for fear of making a creaking sound, and where things were placed, and what they were for. Four rooms stacked simply, one after the other. Front door, living room, Miss Pearl's bedroom, Ham and Wally's room, kitchen, back door. No hallways, just doorways leading from each room in progression. It had been Miss Pearl's mother's mother's home and its furnishings had cradled the members of her family for years. Beneath select floorboards were cavities where a child, like Ham, or like Miss Pearl had been, could still find a charmed or hexed trinket, a magical object left no telling how long ago: a drawstring velvet sachet full of human hair or animal teeth or old coins. In the parlor was a cane that Miss Pearl would sometimes threaten to beat Ham or Wally with, though she never made good on her promise.

To the blue shotgun house a baptism of sorts: may you be washed clean, washed through and through, may the many rushing waters crown you and fill you, may you be purified in spirit, may you live.

II.

WHAT IS RESTORED

1. In which Ham assumes a hero's stride

On the morning after they'd had the same dream, Ham didn't wake Mayfly before getting up to scavenge the kitchen for some breakfast. Even though Mayfly had opened her home to him, he tried to minimally take from her supplies, and now he was cooing at his hunger the way you'd coo at a wild beast, assuring his hunger that it would find some, if not all, of the satisfaction it was looking for. While holding his breath so as not to stir Mayfly from her stone-cold sleep, he shifted his weight on the sofa where he'd found himself upon jolting awake at the sun's light on his face.

As he pulled a cardboard cylinder of oatmeal from her pantry, he heard Mayfly snort in the next room as her first waking inhale came roughly into her sinuses. Shit, he thought.

"Is that you, Ham?" Mayfly called into the kitchen.

"It's me. Don't worry," Ham called back.

"What in the world are you doing?"

"Boiling some oatmeal. Do you want some?"

"I think I'm close enough to you, Ham, without having to stare at you over breakfast."

"Oh," Ham said. Did she think he was some kind of filthy, that the stench of him would rub off on her? She didn't smell so great herself.

"That's not what I mean. Just usually it takes me a while after I wake up before I can really deal with people like that. I'm just going to go out for some coffee. You're charming."

"That's not true, I'm not."

"You are." Mayfly stretched her arms over her head and yawned and then swung her feet around to the edge of the sofa to slip on her flip-flops. She rose and pulled the hoodie, heaped on a chair, over her head.

"I'm out," she said, throwing up the two-fingered peace sign. She didn't stop to consider that Ham, who she should have known was a major coffee drinker, might like to come with her.

Ham knew he was one of a tribe because he had run into others like himself three times in Atlanta.

The first was an older man. It was the first week of Ham's arrival to the city. Ham had walked to the mall in Mayfly's neighborhood, intending to sit on a bench there and watch people pass. He could have seen from a mile away the skittishness in this man's bearing, how the eyes in his face moved like tadpoles in a stream, darting toward the light to be warmed by it and backing away from it again in fear just as quickly—little living lightning flashes.

Ham knows that you can run to outpace trouble on a broken leg; the shock will carry you to safety with superhuman grace. It's only after you get there, to the place where you can rest, that wounds begin to offer themselves to your inspection, and only in their own time. Some cry out to you loudly and cannot be ignored; others wait their turn. These will show you their ways weeks later, or years.

So he had nodded at the older man, passingly, he hoped. He wasn't looking to be approached by him, but once the stranger had gotten his signal—had been glimpsed in the face and taken for a man, that is—he didn't have a second thought before making his way to Ham across the granite floor.

"What part of the city were you from?"

And Ham gave the name of the ward where he'd spent most of his childhood, not the one he had lived in most recently, where dread finally threw off all its disguises.

"And when did you get here?"

"About a week ago."

"Family?"

Ham shook his head. There were no telephone numbers exchanged. Who could remember a new one yet? Who stayed in a home whose host wouldn't be troubled by one extra mouth at the table?

"Take care then," was what the man had said, turning so

that Ham watched the numbers printed on the back of the man's jersey-style shirt wiggle away at the shuffled pace of his gait.

Next it was a teenage girl. This was more than a month into his time in the city, a month of taking up space in Mayfly's house. Mayfly did not seem to care or notice whether he lifted a finger to help. But he thought the least he could do was help fill her refrigerator, so he took a week to rustle up the motivation, finally heaved himself off the sofa, and went to apply for a food-stamps debit card one day.

He singled out this girl on the train on his way to the government office. She was with a flock of girls her own age, but she had not mastered their ways of carrying themselves. It wasn't just her clothes, that her pants bagged where the girls' pants clung to every incipient curve on their young bodies. Or that this girl wore no jewelry, the tiny holes in her earlobes that might have held earrings looking just like the shriveled wounds they were, while the other girls she was riding with were heavily laden with two-dollar plastic baubles that jangled in time with their words.

One of this girl's shoulders slumped lower than the other, and it gave the appearance that she was tilted along a different axis than the planet's, had been thrown off-balance. Like the man at the mall, she approached him first. She asked him if he wanted to get off the train with them at Five Points. Then she said suddenly, "Where you from?"

Above the hulking metal rattle of the train and the animated conversation of the other riders—the two babies crying at opposite ends of the car, the woman in a fast-food uniform venting her day's frustrations not only into her cell phone but across the car into any listening ear, the passengers talking among the people they had come with, the lone travelers jumping into any conversation that sounded appetizing or sympathetic—he learned that this girl had grown up in a neighborhood a few blocks from where he had been born. Her name was Penny. She and her mother were staying with an aunt here. "See you around," she said as she slipped out of the train at her stop, became enfolded by the gaggle of Atlanta girls, and was carried by the wave of them off the platform and up the escalator. But she wouldn't, of course. See him around.

Now Ham's eyes are blinded by the fluorescent lights at the rest stop in Alabama. When Ham steps away from the shelter over the gas station, the night is purple washed, not one star visible. He's traveled all this way from Mayfly's Atlanta duplex and those days are behind him now, just like the years he spent with Miss Pearl, and he wonders if it will be worth fully tuning his senses to this new setting or if it, too, will be fleeting. Fleeting like those moments with the members of his tribe.

From a conversation with a friend of his, the only number Ham had memorized, his whole neighborhood back home was underwater. He stands astride the concrete and I stretch out his limbs, trying on a hero's pose. If he needs galoshes, if he needs a boat, he will return, just to look the act of god in the eye: just to see that such things really do still occur. Jerusalem or whatnot really does get wrecked by god's wrath. God always sent prophets in those days to warn that by sin, one would get wrecked; one would have been sold into slavery by captors. This time, no warning. A weather report. No word from the heavens on who had sinned, whether it was the foreigner or the people of the city. Neither do I have anything to offer in this regard.

Ham has choices to make: whether to press on toward a home in ruins or to take stock of what he has and rest here for a while. In his pocket he fingers the worn paper where he'd written Deborah's number. Deborah, the girl he'd met on that frantic journey out of his city, the girl who'd let him stay in her family's house. It's an option, if he must. Ham considers Deborah's home just outside Morrisville a pitstop until he can earn or borrow enough money to make it home, where he will play the intrepid explorer, travel in canoes down canals that were streets. Save someone else's life if not his own. Pick up someone else's life if not his own. This leaving his hometown has caused him to remember old lessons: that life is a thing that can fly up into the air one moment, that it can resettle the next, that you don't have to be where you were or who you were from one year to another.

Yet he'd been given the perfect opportunity to flutter like a seed into some other furrow, to grow new roots. He could have reinvented himself as anyone. He could have managed to live the same shiftless life he'd been living in any number of cities, leaving one job for another as it suited him, leaving one warm body for another, leaving one history for another. Why else have any of the bus's travelers chosen to return (and if they've gotten this far, they've already returned)? It was not only to obey a human need to survey the damage of their lives, to muck around in the wreckage, hoping to reassemble its brightly colored and metallic ends as if they were magpies. It was to satisfy another tug, too, even more basic: the call homeward, the need to call somewhere home. Why, when home drags you in its dust, when it uproots and disclaims you, and when home spews you out like Jonah ejected from the whale's belly, will you still crawl back? The devil you know, it has long been said, among these exiles and those before them, is better than the devil you don't.

So he finds himself midway to home, in the middle of nowhere, crawling back to what he knows, crawling at a pace he can manage. The winds of night blow over fields and fields of corn and reach him standing on the concrete, sending his senses information about where he stands on the earth. The smell of smoke from trash fires burning a few miles away reaches him and mingles with the gasoline and car exhaust here, where vehicles and people stop to get their bearing, to make their next move, leaving no traces of themselves in these lands they pass through and only stopping when they pass one another long enough to see that they were dispersed from the same place, uprooted by the same disaster, unwitting members of the same diaspora.

2. In which the arrow of Ham's compass arrives at a temporary resting place

At the rest stop, the night is still purple washed. He is five hours away from Atlanta now, two hours from where he used to call home, and either place could easily be a universe away from where he stands.

Many miraculous things occur while buses are stalled. Decisions are made that move people from one stage of life to another. At filling stations late at night, it is rare but not unheard of for people to abandon the journey altogether in favor of the city where they're stopped or to reroute toward somewhere they've never been. It is not at all uncommon for someone to develop the kind of resolve while a bus is stopped that allows them to forge a relationship with a difficult family member where none at all was possible. People accept and decline jobs over the phone when buses are stopped. Sharing a soft drink and stretching their arms, folks make new friends with people who had been sitting somewhere else on the bus, the kind of friends you resolve to stay in touch with once you each descend at your final destination, although you never do end up speaking again, pivotal as that four-hour relationship was, as much as your life was changed by it. There is something about the sudden intrusion of false daylight in the fluorescent lights overhead, something about the feeling of being nowhere in particular on the map, suspended somewhere in the vast, irrelevant landscape between where you're going and where you're coming from. Certain things become possible that were not otherwise.

There's a feeling he has, a feeling only a bit of age can inspire in us about home: that he does not return to the same place. It will be altered, it will be a new sphere superimposed on the old. These are the kinds of newnesses Ham can ready himself for: new worlds upon old worlds. How when he'd moved somewhere new as a child, or been new, he would visit the street he'd formerly lived on. And though in his mind he could make out that every door on the street was the same door it had always been, the street would have changed now that he could no longer call it his own.

Ham begins to mark the faces of the other passengers as he stands on solid ground again in line for the payphone, finding distant kin in them. That old woman who sits on the curb, wiry white strands flying free of her plait, becomes his grandmother's sister. He imagines that once when he was a small kid he had been stung by a bee on a visit to her house in the country, and she had taken him on her knee to calm him before setting him down to scrape the stinger out of the skin on his arm, then cooling the wound with ice.

They have been set back in time, these displaced ones. Rootless, they are often resigned to use the last of the world's payphones, machines sulking at odd corners in rusted neglect and defaced by chewing gum or graffiti or grime on every surface. Before leaving his cell phone behind in the flood, the last time he had pushed coins into metal slots might have been as a kid at those toy machines in the front of the supermarket, so that every call he made on a payphone still filled him with the thrilling subliminal anticipation of a shiny prize. It was this if he could not beg for a few minutes on the cell phone of a compassionate stranger.

To tell himself, as he did, that he hadn't considered Deborah often since he'd left her home almost two months ago was less than true. Truer was that he didn't know what to consider her as. People had clung to him before. He had shaken some of them off, and others, like me, he'd allowed to seize some part of him, fallen under their shadows for some period of time. He could do his share of clinging too, but he was inclined to cling to what resisted him or eluded him, cling to the hope of it. What wanted him, if it had not the strength to overpower him completely in its pursuit, he resisted.

There were Deborah's ordinary details: medium height so the top of her head nested just under his chin if they stood belly-to-belly, broad-set eyes that trusted everything they saw, skilled hands with long fingers looking for something to care for. The imitation perfume she wore, bought from a kiosk at the mall in

Mobile, a smell that would rub off on him and had become the predominant scent of his days at her family's house. He hadn't asked for her to become a part of his life—how often do we get to specifically request the people we'd like to enter our knowledge— but she had become so anyway. She had been his guide out of the entire world as he used to know it. He could hold her, the event of having met her, responsible for the fact that nothing was as he knew it and he was set adrift in strange lands. He could hold her responsible for the fact that despite his resistance, he might still need her.

And forgive Ham for still puzzling over Mayfly, not Deborah, as he stands at the rest stop. He has puzzled over her for years, mused over her ability to take life into her own hands as though it were a silk ribbon. Even as a young boy he was certain that this power would never be his. Mayfly was born into privilege, and every deliberate move she made garnered her even greater privilege. He could not say whether such freedom was of this world or not, but he knew, at least, that it was not of his world. Not today, not anymore, receding, as it had always tended to recede, from his reach.

Ham thinks about shelter. An instinct kicks in. He doesn't want to think of Deborah as something like home, even though it was through her home that he'd wandered, zombie-like, until he could flee to Atlanta. He'd wanted to dismiss the details of her as unremarkable, that medium build and the way she held herself as though begging, her straightened hairstyle that was always subject to change if there was a way she could fashion herself that would be more pleasing to the gaze of others. He suspected her of wanting more from him than he could give. But he strengthens himself by drawing up his shoulders. We can get free of her if we need to, we can get in and get out. He can't think of a hospitable place for him in his hometown. It's only a way station.

The phone Ham borrows after abandoning hope of getting at the payphone—he has no legitimate hurry but obeys the compulsion of the inertia pent up in his limbs from sitting still for so long—belongs to a woman old enough to be his mother. A few years younger than Miss Pearl, perhaps, in a shirt screen-printed with the long, warped face and the birth and death dates of a loved one. Thanking her, Ham dials, encouraged by her hand and its carefully tended nails waving no trouble, it's nothing. A female voice he knows answers. "Hey," he says in reply to her sleepy greeting.

"Is this Hamilton?" she asks, her voice startled to anxious enthusiasm. "Did you make it to Atlanta?"

"I made it back."

"To where? Here?" and when Ham mumbles his affirmation, "Well, come on then. We all missed you. Come home."

That word, *home*, insisted on: "Come home, we need you here."

"Need me for what?" Ham says dubiously.

"Hamilton." Turning the corners of the word downward so it wasn't his name but an admonition.

"I mean I have nothing, is all."

"No, you have us. And we need you. Especially now. Come

on and let me talk to you. There's something you need to know."
He thinks she's biting her bottom lip. "I mean what are you going
to do, go back? To what?"

"Yeah, I could," he says, indignant. "It's my home."

"Everyone misses you here. Everyone was worried sick about
you."

"I told you where I was going."

"You never called."

"I'm calling now. I took the bus down. We're at the rest stop
not far from y'all."

"So come on. Ellis can be there in forty-five minutes."

Ham glances toward the lady to whom the phone belongs.
She is still looking at him reassuringly, not eager to hound him
about his time, not giving him the excuse he's looking for to hang
up. But he needs to squelch the uneasiness Deborah's voice has
raised in him, so he tells her anyway, "Let me call you back. This
nice lady let me use her phone and I don't want to take all her
minutes."

The bus that had carried him all this way begins to board, but
Ham finds himself bound to his word and to the concrete, and
he finds his legs carrying him to the payphone outside the convenience store, the line now dispersed. It is in no small part due to
my influence that he grips the receiver, which squeaks like rubber
against his palm. He places it against the skin of his check, where
it is ice cool, and he returns the phone call he had dropped earlier.
The pleading voice that had met him not long ago resumes its
entreaty, now turning coy. "Seemed to me like if you'd wanted to,
you could have stayed there, could have stayed with your friend.

So I know you must have wanted to come back to us. You have nowhere else to go," Deborah tells him.

The young girl he'd shared a seat with on the way from Atlanta flattens her palm against the window from inside the bus, its fleshier parts pressed a bloodless white. Ham, no longer at eye level with the passengers, now looking up at them in their seats behind glass high above him for the first time, sees the gesture of her small hand as a goodbye. He hears himself as I assent to spending just this one night with Deborah and her tribe of brothers, conceding to her that he owns no property to be salvaged back home and is neither brave nor strong enough to save the lives of others. That the landscape will not be what he's known. Could be that he surrenders to the realization that it might so cripple him to see what nature has made of the town that he'd be of no use to anyone but himself, that he might be just as lost wandering in a city whose streets had become rearranged as he was in the strange worlds beyond it.

3. In which two men and a dog ride into the stars

Ham sits on the curb outside the convenience store, lodged between the gloomy lump of his backpack and a bicycle rack. At a time like this, in a pocket of solitude, when the nearest human being is not within sight—for the man who lords over the convenience store in a stained polo shirt has dipped into some closet or back room and all the warmth of Ham's body has by now escaped the seat he'd once occupied on that bus traveling steadily closer to home and farther from him—he could see himself trying to love Deborah. It seems that Deborah is the most recently convenient object to place over the threadbare loneliness that reveals itself to Ham from time to time, as one might move a rug, chair, or table to cover a stain on the floor. Moments like this, while Ham drifts far away, I slip into his skin like a hand into a glove. I stretch him around, kicking the legs and the arms.

In this moment, as Ham tries love of Deborah on for size, her brother Ellis shuttles toward him from the house some twenty miles away. He pulled out of the driveway, the tires of the pickup truck spitting gravel, a soft drink fizzling in the red plastic cup at his side, the dog pacing the back seat, wobbling against the vehicle's motion to make a bed for himself. Ellis has come to a begrudging acceptance of the fact that Ham is family. Perhaps the kind of family that is made, not born; water thick enough with sediment to approximate the weight of blood. Chief among the values Ellis has inherited and shares with all his siblings is a feudal fidelity to kith and kin. Another of their shared values—one that has stood many tests—is love of the land, whether they are owned by the land or whether they own it.

It was late at night when Ham first came to them, dragged by Deborah, who had fled his hometown's chaos with him. Ham's and Deborah's faces were ravaged, expressions wiped from them cleanly by the wind. When they'd arrived at her family's house across two state lines, their clothes had clung to them with the sweat and grime of a day and a half. Ham was shown the bathroom, where he remembers barricading himself for hours, letting the water bear into him long after it had run cold. When he came out, Deborah had her turn at the shower while he sat with her brothers in the living room and scratched their compliant, sad-eyed brown dog behind the ears. The TV, muted, silently cast its colored lights on the dark shag carpet, broadcasting images of the storm and its wake Ham was numb to.

Ellis and Deborah live in the same house, ostensibly to care for their father, Bo, in his old age—though Bo, despite his potbelly, can still walk for many miles without stopping for breath and still possesses the uncanny ability to take apart any mechanical object, clock or car, leave the pieces in one oily metallic heap, and assemble them a few days later in better working order than they'd been to begin with. Though Bo's youngest son, Reed, is fighting the good fight thousands of miles away in a battered desert town, he is always present in their home, if only because he watches everything they do from a photograph in a spot of honor on the living room mantel, cast dapper and courageous in his military uniform. Their brother Arthur, Ham learned, doesn't live with Ellis and Deborah but down the road with his wife and stepchild. He comes by every night after the rest of them have eaten and are relaxing, makes himself a small plate of cold food, and takes his place on the sofa next to Ellis.

That first night in Deborah's narrow bed, the room pitch dark save for a thin line of light that came under the door, Deborah curled tightly around him, a python, and he did not protest when the will of his body gave way to hers. Ellis's rattling snores on the other side of the wall tunneled their way into Ham's dreams as a helicopter hummed overhead.

Now, under his sister's instructions, Ellis is chewing up the dotted yellow line that divides the highway with his truck and spitting it into his rearview. Night, or some force that matches its power, has slammed into the landscape, flattening everything. Tall grasses with bent backs and old houses with wood worn to gray appear out of the darkness under the beam of his headlights. Poststorm houses as he draws closer to the Gulf Coast, cocked and leaning, tipping sideways, shredded, often reduced to piles of splinter and rubble; sometimes there is only a barren stoop where a whole house might have been. Ellis passes concrete basketball courts without baskets. The odd letter is missing from businesses along the highway: LEON VE TABLE. Ellis sings along with the radio in a nasal voice, very nearly in tune. For all his life, the dog has had only one facial expression available to him: a skeptical one. In the back seat he lets his eyes loll to his master's song and raises the skin where his eyebrows might have been.

Waiting, Ham fingers the tiny pendant where a miniature fragment of my bone, set behind velvet and enclosed within a bubble of glass, the talisman no bigger than a fingernail, hangs around a pewter chain. He vacates: I look through his eyes, I operate his feet as he stomps a small rhythm.

Back when I was growing up, the map of the world had not yet come to settle into the form that Ham knows now. Up and down were still contested directions. The map's center was not fixed. Sea monsters curled their tails and tossed their heads above the water's surface at the ends of the ocean, lying in wait for those who wandered off the edge of the world's known bounds. The southern continent of America was amorphous, its undetermined shape growing sharper every few years. Any two points on the globe could draw closer together than they were now or could drift farther apart at the will of god.

The cities of the Incas were still inhabited, if sparsely, by the people whose grandfathers had built them, though the spirit of the grandfathers had disinherited them and left them godless. They hobbled toward the love of Christ, who accepted them with open arms as he accepts us all.

In the hundred years that passed between the time Atahualpa's head was roasted by the Spaniards and the time my own lifeless body was partitioned—my bones nicked so that shards of them could be sent to far corners of the earth, my clothes shredded so that churches could be founded on their pieces—some worlds had met their end, others had begun, others had collided with one another. Common languages were broken between generations; the words of the father no longer suited the son. It's still this way, more than ever. Since my day, when the plug was released, the endless suck of time down its drain approaches greater speed with every year that passes. The world of the son drifts exponentially away from the world of the father. No words between them can bridge the ever-widening gap.

Ham is working under a new map himself. Since his world has gone in a thousand directions, his map is no longer limited by the bounds of the city where he was born. His map of that city is most intricate; each street not only has a name but is garlanded with the blossoms of history. But now there is a hazy view of parts of the world progressively north and east of his city, and there is the knowledge that the intricate sphere of his city is but a small dot in the scheme of things, if a bright and beckoning one. The second point to appear on his new map represents Deborah's house, to the north and to the east of home. This is a point that launched him to, and now called him from, the third point to appear on the new map: Atlanta, farther to the north and farther to the east of Deborah. Having seen with his own eyes that a real city with its own dialect and smells fills this point gives him the possibility of a proper place for Mayfly in his mind. If he would let her, she could now become more than the phantom of the past that she has been for him. As it is, he cannot abide an earthly home for her. So there was no room for him in Atlanta.

Too soon, the light of Ellis's truck shoots into Ham's eyes, and he is blind for a painful instant. Ellis leaves the engine running and hops out to greet Ham, lifting him off the ground in a sound hug with a groan. Back on his feet, Ham lifts his backpack by one strap, opens the passenger side of the truck, and climbs into its elevated cabin. The dog clambers over to him from the back seat, happy to see him, and rests his head in Ham's lap the whole way.

"You been okay?" Ellis asks when they have sealed the vehicle against the rush of night.

"Yeah, you?"

"Alright," Ellis says, mouth pressed.

The landscape illuminated in the tunnel of Ellis's headlights unfolds like the tape of a catastrophe played in reverse as the two men and their dog roll back inland; houses and fences rise from their ruins to become whole again. Their truck is stalked by a moon that keeps its distance, lest it call too much attention to itself. How often I feel like the man in that moon.

Deborah's was the first world Ham had been a part of since he had left home. She had ferried him away from all he had ever known, across one of those fabled rivers of no return: Rubicon, Styx, Mississippi. He first saw her spotlighted under an incandescent billboard that advertised Jax, the long-obsolete beer for which Ham and the other residents of his hometown were given a phantom craving, a taste no earthly balm could satisfy. It was on neutral ground where they met, in the middle of the street in the city that was itself a canal that carried a steady current of people and their cars and at night became a stream of lights. Deborah was lost, a country girl bewildered by its brightness. She had come to Ham's city from her home for a hair show and had lost the friends she'd traveled down there with.

"I got to get out of here," she had stopped Ham to say. She had caught Ham by the sleeve of his windbreaker, eyes wild with panic. This was the beginning of the one howling endless night that became more than one day, across which Ham and Deborah would make their frenzied exodus with the rest of the throng that tumbled out of the city and dispersed in every direction, many of them never to return to the streets that were the landscape of their memories.

Deborah's family's home near Morrisville was Ham's whole sphere for two strange weeks that were no more real to Ham now than if they had been dreamed. It was a slow process of waking up since leaving his home. He'd stared, zombie-like, at the television with the others for hours every day, and images of his destroyed town flashed before them silently, banners of text rolled beneath to call them to highest drama. Though he was not asked, he took on a few household chores. He washed dishes a couple nights, finding a kernel of delight in the way the family's plates sat on the rack when he was done, bone-clean and steaming, so polished that a finger squeaked as it ran across one. He let the dog out if the dog scratched at the screen door while he was in the kitchen. He took the dog for a walk, once. Got on his knees in the bathroom the second day to scrub the tub with all the fight left in him. He roasted peanuts in the oven and shared them with the family. Each day he became more real to himself than he had been the day before. He worked hard to avoid Deborah's gaze by day, which would have told him more than he wanted to know about either of them. Nevertheless, he reached for her at night or allowed himself to be reached for, warmed by the fire that throbbed somewhere within her and made her skin hot to the touch. He ignited something secret in her. He took a secret pleasure, knowing this, and kept the secret from himself. His body began to feel more like his own, and the one who looked at him from behind the mirror grew more familiar, until one day—the day he got into the car that would carry him to Mayfly in Atlanta—he could fearlessly stare into his own reflected eyes. Before, it might have been me who looked back.

Ham clicks opens the door of Ellis's blue truck, and the dog runs out before them, thumping its tail with pleasure. It takes several waves of the animal's tail to disperse the old vision to mist. And it is clear that the house where Deborah lives was not a dreamed house but a real one. As to what Deborah carries in the ever-so-slight but firmly rounded paunch that she shoves at Ham from across the doorstep to exaggerate its curve, there can be no doubt.

4. In which the secrets of the womb are revealed

The cold rain in Atlanta had inspired him, for the first time in his life, to dream of spring. He had felt cold enter his fingers in a way he'd never known and felt it enter his feet. Felt cold as a thing to defend against and seek refuge from. And, growing callous to the cold, he had honed the exquisite anticipation of a warmth he had known before that surely would return. He'd discovered that a person could incubate a guaranteed hope that things would be better. Maybe then they would get worse, but then they would be better again. The cold has already left him, but this odd new faith stays: a rooted belief in the revolution of the planet and in the sureness of the centered sun that only waits for him to come around to it.

He has returned under the cover of night to the pale-yellow house he left two months ago. It isn't a large house from the outside, but inside it has the feeling of great space and warmth. The front door where they enter, which leads off the porch, is almost never used. It opens to a foyer where no footsteps ever fall, where pretty green and blue and crystal glass pieces, the wedding gifts of three generations, are displayed. It is Deborah who keeps this room free of dust, a living memorial, where ancestors look out from their picture frames with the faintest traces of smiles on their dignified sepia faces. The walls in the den are paneled vertically in pinewood, the sofas there shielded from the mess of life by clear plastic covers from which it could be painful to unstick one's sweaty thighs in the summer.

How different the house is since Ham last saw it. He knows it hasn't really changed, but he has learned from the many different houses in which he's slept over the course of his years how a room will bend through the prism of familiarity—that the walls of small spaces expand and that harsh colors fade. Nooks and corners will open themselves and bare their contents. Dust will make itself visible, but distinct smells that had once been easy to make out will eventually fade into unconscious impression. Whatever the inhabitants have erected as monuments to their prosperity will be revealed as just that; so the large, flat, shiny television in the corner of the living room will stand out now more than ever to Ham when he makes his way into the living room from the kitchen. I walk Ham through the house, remembering.

Deborah leads the way through the living room to the kitchen at the back of the house, where she resumes shaving patterns into the hair of a neighbor. The hairstyle she gives him, which had been popular around the time Ham was born, is recently back in fashion. It allowed a man's hair to progress in length and thickness from near-bald around the skull's base—where it could become a canvas for the geometric designs of one's heart's content—to full and high over the top.

It isn't this style that Ham asks for. After placing his backpack in the living room and admiring the television exactly as he'd known he would, Ham returns to the kitchen. The neighbor has gone home satisfied and Deborah is resting a little against the sink, exchanging pleasantries with her brother. Ham waits and listens unfocused to the soothing lilt of the banter between the pair who had practiced their first words on each other. Then he asks for his cut and poises himself on the stool as Deborah stands above him with her electric razor.

Travel-weary Ham is easier for me to manipulate. His choice to return to Deborah's home was its own surrender and its own defeat, and, coupled with the strain of the journey, it makes it easier for me to turn Ham's head this way and that for her, arrange his limp and compliant hands in his lap. And I'll dare to plant a thought, words coming from a place he doesn't know but knows he can't take responsibility for: *I'm staying here. I rest here.*

At his feet the hair falls like black cotton, soft and silent upon the floor. The air in the kitchen refreshes his scalp; now he knows what Mayfly was talking about that time. He feels a little like he's captured one key on the ring of her secrets.

Deborah's hand is steady and professional. She's been in and out of beauty school for her certification but has been known for fixing the hair of young and old since she was a child. It's only by relying on what her hands know of their own accord that she is able to rise above the wild sea of what she feels toward Ham at this moment, to move steadily, hands at a remove from the anger and the yearning that stirs her heartbeat to a frenzied pounding in her ears. The fact that she holds a weapon against his skin thrills her so much that she doesn't know how she contains the electricity, how she keeps the moment from tipping over into violence. But it's a testament to the strict discipline she was raised with that she is able to hold any emotion that might trouble Ham away from him, protect him from herself, swallow the flames that rage in her.

When she finishes and stands admiring her handiwork and the perfection it reveals in the shape of Ham's head, Deborah says, "Shiny-bald wouldn't suit you, Hamilton. So I'll leave just a layer between you and the sky."

He scoots around to face her, and she hands him a mirror. She says in one burst while Ham admires himself, as if it might be the only chance she has, "I guess you can figure things out."

"I know how to keep my hair, nothing to it."

"You know exactly what I'm talking about."

He doesn't, of course, nor does he want to. Ham sets his right foot on the floor, prepared to propel himself off the stool, but Deborah grabs him by the arm, startling him more by the moxie than by the strength of her gesture. He knows it took a lot of dammed-up will for her to take hold of him like that. And she pulls his arm toward the very small, very firm rounding of her belly and presses it there. If Deborah had not been bird-thin, so concave that the richest of meals left her unsatisfied, there might have been nothing for Ham to feel there in the pit of her belly.

"It's mine?" he asks, stalling for time while the wheels in his mind spin his thoughts beyond capture.

"It's mine," Deborah says.

"Good, keep it that way."

"Yours too, though."

"I'm not marrying nobody."

"Nobody asked you to."

Somewhere behind his inclination toward denial, beneath the rigidity that had taken hold of his body in these moments since Deborah had forced him to confront her, the hope of the spring months and their warmth and green is rising—or it had already risen—and like a climbing spring vine has now found something to latch onto.

In a last protest before this hope sunk its teeth into him: "I'm too young."

"Old enough, Ham." She shoves his arm away and with her electric razor motions for him to get down.

"Now you, Daddy," she says, loud enough for Bo to amble in from the next room and take his place on the stool Ham had warmed for him.

"Careful with this old head of mine, darling," Bo says above the din of crickets crouched low in the cool grass outdoors whose slow voices had peaked and could be heard even through the glass.

5. In which possessions are taken hold of

Yawning water, exhaling it; swallowing water, passing water through its tissue-transparent body, the child who already possesses Ham's forehead drifts into a somersault, a slow and private turning. It is in a unique limbo, material part of a world from which it's hidden, suspended and isolated, within but above. From a minute blackberry-puckered cluster, it had danced itself out into Precambrian shrimp shapes and has only recently assumed the intricate form of a very tiny human being. Most of what it has known had been created alongside it and in support of its survival. Even the water—vital water, nourishing water that conducts the sure metronomic whispers of distant mother-organs and the sound of the mother-voice that vibrates, soothes, or startles its world, her body. The child lies in perfect darkness, perfect warmth, and it

floats in waters in which it is the only thing that ever moves or is
moved, as our creator had in his own first days.

It thinks of nothing. There is nothing to think of and there
is nothing to be wanted. Deborah's emotions are its elements. It
is agitated by mother-stress, relaxed by mother-calm, as a plant
tilts its head toward the sun and opens its pores for the moon.
Deborah is learning what it's like to be claimed by another as
territory. She is all the terrain the blind child floating in darkness
can know; she has been seized by its spirit, her body co-opted in
service to its demands. It has staked itself as a tiny flag, marking
its own.

The child knows little yet about the family of which it is a
part—only an inkling of those things Deborah knows she cannot
articulate herself—and Ham doesn't know much more about the
family than the child does. He knows that they are hospitable
people, and he knows that he feels apart from them. He knows
their last name—Everett—not because it had ever become rele-
vant to conversation but because he'd made it out on the mailbox
when he pulled away last time.

Ham wakes up in the night gasping for breath, as though his
dreams have tried to drown him. He rises, leaving Deborah alone
in the twin bed. Hand on his chest, beneath the cold tin medal
bearing my image—this is a new feeling for him, the wind snagged
on his lungs as he tries to push it from his body. By moonlight he
finds the pair of his jeans he'd draped on the bedroom's only chair,
pulls them over his taut bare legs, and stumbles, gasping, into the

kitchen. Opens the tap, sticks his head under, and guzzles water straight from the faucet. This seems to help. Calmed, he takes a glass and fills it with water, and while he stands by the back door's window the column of water in his hand holds the light of the moon. His thoughts join the howling of the dog outside, who has tilted his head to let moonlight pour down his parched throat and to beg of heaven.

Of course Ham thinks of slipping out the door. The night does call so—calls audibly. His rambling muscle, which had lain much of the past few years in atrophy, stayed flexed these days, kept at the ready. His possessions are fewer than they've ever been, and there's nothing that can't be replaced. He wanders to the table where someone had placed his backpack to set his glass of water down, unzips the backpack and roots around, feeling the toothpaste, toothbrush, the rolled-up undershirts. The comfort in the feel of the cheap, worn cotton is twofold: it's all in there, but he could get by without it.

He doesn't hear the padded step of a much larger (much lighter-footed) man down the hallway, so he's got a look of startled red-handed betrayal on his face when Ellis appears beside him at the table.

"You couldn't sleep either" are Ellis's words.

Ham tells him, "It's some moon." No lie. It was one omniscient bloodshot eyeball.

Ellis's bulk is buried in the flowing folds of the gray sweatpants he sleeps in, and he makes no sound as he moves to the stove until he speaks. "I was going to put some milk on, like Mama used to do for us when we couldn't sleep. Works like a charm."

Ham backs away slightly from the word *Mama* and its invitation to imagine Ellis, Deborah, or anybody else as a child, but he is willing to accept the mug of thick sweetened milk Ellis sets before him.

"You just left a little something in your bag, huh?"—Ellis's voice takes on a suggestive hypnotism—"And then you just had to admire the moon a little. That right? Because we're sure glad to have you with us, Ham. We hope you'll stay awhile. See out your obligations and what have you. Do you have plans?"

"Plans?"

"Work plans, something?"

Ham lets the milk's froth coat his upper lip and distracts himself with its sensation. He looks at the very faint hairs that bridge Ellis's eyebrows, a way of focusing a gaze somewhere near Ellis's fierce eyes without meeting them.

"Yeah, well, you can think about that. You can just try thinking about that." I can pluck an implied *motherfucker* out of the breath behind this, the edge of a threat at which Ham flinches and looks away.

"Listen, I know you had it rough," Ellis continues. "We can find something for you to do, but you have to do something. This just isn't going to work. I mean this," he pounds the table flathanded, rattling it and disturbing the calm milk in Ham's mug, "this all costs something. Somebody has worked hard for all this."

"I know. It's . . . I'm grateful and all."

It is difficult for Ham to see himself as Ellis sees him and until now he had never tried. It hurts a little bit for him to do so, but he goes as far into the territory as he can before self-preservation forces him to turn back: a young man, not too much mass to him and not enough years to amount to much, city sullied but not citified, alien and low-class and strange-talking when he did talk, silent when words were called for, pitiful and pitiable, an undeserving beneficiary of Ellis's family's grace and his sister's love. Was there any point to disproving all this—was there the possibility?

With a napkin from the table, Ellis dabs the moon-illuminated sweat that has formed on his forehead. "Now I've upset myself. And you too. When what we both need to do is sleep."

The tightness that first woke him returns to Ham's chest. The ragged, torn breath that comes into him is squeezed out reluctantly by lungs that want to suck all they can from it, that doubt its return, missing the air before it's gone. I need Ham's breath, so I am as alarmed as he is by the new sensations.

"I like you, Ham," Ellis says, rising from his chair to clink his mug into the sink, to leave Ham alone. "I like you. But it's not just charm that's going to get you through. You got to man up."

His light shuffle disappears down the hall. And now even the dog outdoors, which Ham thinks of as his closest ally in the household, is asleep. Now that Ellis has left him, he has for company the moon with which this kitchen is awash, his thoughts, and me.

Ham knows by now that I watch him. It's dawned on him sometime over the years—he feels the trace of my gaze. When, like earlier today, he's riding in a car and feels someone looking at him, he knows that while the eyes of the other drivers capsuled in their cars are on the road and their passengers' attentions are held by conversations with one another or cast downward at devices in their laps, still he is watched. The feeling—you know it too—is that a light shines on him, though there is no heat to it and no radiance. It's not quite an itch, but it's a clear tug: the signal that travels down invisible lines from our eyes toward whatever we have cast them on. We know if someone watches us; even I can remember this much of what it is to be flesh. It's to be pulled by invisible forces—rather than to be yourself invisible, pulled toward the weight and gravity of living bodies and their fragments, toward the far-flung fragments of what was your own body.

Yes, Ham carries such a fragment of my body with him at all times, a tiny pebble made of my bone, inside a little glass bubble set in a metal pendant. A single point from which my presence, for him, once radiated, though by now I'm throughout him. By now, I can freely observe from inside him and sometimes even move him as I will, if it's best. At times when he's weary and willing to surrender, Ham can feel me move through him like a current.

Whether Ham in Deborah's kitchen moves his own limbs or whether I relieve him of the effort, he does find his way back to bed after Ellis has left him alone, does find his place next to Deborah, and, like the child nestled within her, rides the sound of her breath into bottomless sleep.

6. In which the lotus is eaten

Ham enjoys the privilege this morning of catching himself in the process of waking before his eyes have opened, so he chooses to hold the moment and draw out his waking slowly, to rest behind his closed eyes and form his impression of the waiting day. To make his predictions of it sight unseen. He draws the outlines of the world around him on the red screen the backs of his eyelids provide him, lit as they are by a sun well on its way to the height of the sky. He traces the room around him, with its one small white chair and small white table—furniture that was too low to the ground to be of much use, not having been built to host occasions more grave than a child's tea party. He can see the bedroom so clearly that he doesn't need to open his eyes yet: how the lace frill on the curtain at the window—also made with a little girl's tastes in mind—catches and filters the morning sun. Sometimes I leave Ham alone for these moments when he is just feeling himself come into his body again.

The wide freedom of the air circulating around him in that bed suggests that the door to the bedroom is open, as do the strong smells and clear sounds of breakfast wafting toward him (a pot of coffee not more than five minutes old, potatoes with black pepper and onions sizzling in the grease of the bacon fried just before them). Deborah no longer weights the bed bedside him, so he stretches his arms and legs wide, feeling them slide into cooler regions of the bedsheets.

On rising, he goes to the kitchen, where Bo is at the stove. Seeing Ham, Deborah gives up her seat at the table. She turns that pleading in her eyes on him when she asks him how he slept. Cocking her head toward Bo while his back is turned, she silently mouths to Ham, *Don't tell.*

Bo leaves his potatoes for a moment to take up the coffeepot, but Deborah gently lifts the pot from his hands to pour the cup herself. "I'll do it, Daddy. He drinks it black, doesn't like a lick of cream."

And she hands the hot cup to Ham, who thanks her sincerely. Enveloped in the warm fragrant cloud of steam over the brim, he asks her, "What day is today?"

He figures that learning what day of the week it is will start him well on the new course that seems to have rolled itself out before him in only the last half a day. It's been quite some time since he's had more than a tenuous grasp on the day of the week or the calendar, and he knows it's become time to do all he can to shake off, at last, the feeling of floating he has had for months now. It strikes him that it is becoming less and less likely that the day will come when he'll take his bag, thank the Everetts for their kindness, bid them farewell forever, and go ahead home never to hear from them again. He is becoming part of them and *if* he escapes—*when*, he cries against himself—it will not be without carrying some piece of them with him, as surely as he has left his piece here, his buried, secret spore.

"Saturday," Bo tells him, his laugh sealed over by the steam rising from the pan. "What day is it where you were, son?"

Bo has set the potatoes aside and is cracking six eggs into the pan, sowing black pepper over the eggs as they determine themselves, quickly turning solid and white where they had been formless and colorless.

Deborah takes a paper plate from a cabinet and stands beside her father as he slides two quivering eggs onto it; then she herself serves it with potatoes and three dark slices of bacon. That's Bo's plate, and after setting it onto the table she takes a paper plate in each of her hands, and Bo flips two more eggs onto each plate and also piles potatoes and bacon onto them, since his hands have become free and Deborah's are occupied. And that's one plate for her and one for Ham.

When they're all seated and Deborah has blessed the food, Bo breaks a yolk with his fork and then mashes the eggs and the potatoes together on his plate, making the meal's inaugural fork strokes, and the three fall into pace together. When Bo says how good it is to have Ham here again and asks if he plans to stay awhile, Deborah turns to look at Ham as expectantly as Bo does.

"I really want to get on home. It's been more than four months now. See if people I know are okay and if I still have a life there," Ham tells them with a fragile resolve.

Against his better judgment, he glances over at Deborah, swallowing her food hard in an attempt to suppress a feeling rising in her. He backtracks. "But you know, I'll stay as long as you'll have me and see if I can pay back what I owe."

"What you owe us? Ham, you don't owe anything."

Ham had long been sure Deborah would have disagreed with such a statement and he now had reason to suspect the same of Ellis, so he couldn't help but be skeptical of this claim of their father's.

"No, y'all have really been so kind to me, and I don't deserve it. I'm not trying to put upon you."

"When somebody needs, we have. It's simple as that, right, Deb?"

"You're family to us, Ham," Deborah says.

"When Deborah brung you to us, it was clear. You were in a bad way. And"—he waves a strip of bacon for emphasis—"whatever we can do we'll still do. When you left you were missed. And now that you're back from . . . where is it?"

"Georgia," Deborah supplied.

"Right. Now that that didn't work out for you, we want to see you doing well somehow."

It's kind of them.

It's kind, too, when Ellis comes home from Mass the next day and finds Ham, who's also just returning from town from a successful quest for some sugarcane to suck on. He tells Ham that there's a job for him if he wants it. Ellis volunteers as a firefighter but makes his living selling farm equipment. They could use some help with collections, he tells Ham. The two sit in the small dining room that is never used for dining, and Ellis presents Ham with the clipboard and preliminary instructions, gives him a badge with his name on it. Ham would have to travel the county, visiting Ellis's clients to settle debts. It seems like a good enough idea; Ham doesn't have any better ones, and as Deborah has put it to him, doesn't he want to have anything to give his child?

Because the reality's congealing around him, and maybe if he'd had more to cling to it would have struck him with less force, this fact that a human creature that he has half-made or at least half-sparked will exist beside him one day in the not-too-distant future. If he plays it right, this person will love him as he's never been loved. Love him as Deborah may never know how, love him as his mother never could love him through the haze of her chemical trance. Love him as his father never did care to love or even know of him, love him as Miss Pearl could have loved him had he never unearned it. Love him as I love him; be a body he can live on in even after his own has worn itself obsolete. Live on in this new body as I live on in him.

Ellis gives him a pair of khaki pants Reed left behind and has Ham try one of his own collared white shirts, which billows embarrassingly around him. He's more Arthur's size, so he's asked to run the long rural block to Arthur's house, wheezing and gasping when he gets to the door. A run's never done that to him before. It's the same feeling he woke with on his first night back here.

In the rising sun of Monday morning, Ham looks at himself in the mirror after shaving. His haircut's still impeccable. He is distinguished in his borrowed clothes. His legs are sturdy enough for a long day of fording dirt driveways, his face stoic enough to endure the doors that will inevitably slam in it.

Ham has had very little experience behind the wheel of a car, though he does carry a tattered Louisiana driver's license, which he'd gone through the trouble of procuring for the sole purpose of legally buying beer. He's been given permission to borrow Arthur's wife's car, a foreign-made machine almost exactly as old as he is. To start it, you have to hit the dashboard hard exactly three times, then turn the ignition just so. Some very sturdy and craftily applied duct tape seals the back-left window.

The first farm he visits grows soybeans. It sprawls some twenty miles away. Twelve Bolivian workers on break—who had made their northern exodus in stages from the same lush, rainy town, where their formerly barefoot children, now inches taller than their fathers have last seen them, are shod in North American sneakers—rise at once from their places in the shade of oak trees that line the gravel drive when they see the little car approach. Turning the car off and taking the key out, Ham rests in the driver's seat for a minute, and he and the men peer at one another with equal curiosity and suspicion, he looking out from his bubble and they looking in from their broad expanse of earth. Ham musters up some authority and gets out.

"Where's the boss?" he asks the one closest, squaring his legs

on the ground. The man, who wears a cap pulled down so low as
to obscure his eyes, is silent.

"Y'heard me? I'm here to talk to the boss."

The man he's speaking to begins to laugh roaringly, and the
others murmur to one another about who this kid thinks he is
in a tongue Ham doesn't speak, a future colloquial dialect of the
language I grew up speaking.

Finally, having surmised that Ham is no threat to them, the
first man steps toward him, puts a plaid-clad arm across his back,
and leads him up the hill to their supervisor in the double-wide
trailer that is his office. When Ham shakes the supervisor's large
red hand, his small brown one is buried in it. "I'm from Grover
and Company," he says, "here to talk about your bill."

The man quickly scratches a number down in ink on a scrap
of pale-yellow paper. "Call this," he says. "We got things to do
around here."

"If they tell you that," Ellis advises Ham at dinner that night,
"you need to make it clear to them that you will not leave until
you speak to someone who handles accounts payable, in person. I
don't care if you have to sit there all day and wait for someone to
drive in from two hours away, don't let them run you around. Try
again tomorrow."

Ham does try the next day, and the day after that, and the
next one. The sunshine is good for him; he can feel it darken and
refine him through the car's glass or directly overhead when, as
the days pass, he stands on soil under which the predestined nubs

of cotton-thorn lay tight, ready to spring, or over which corn has
already sprung, waving at his height. He's beginning to learn the
rhythms of the borrowed car that purrs under him so many hours
a day and the lay of the land. Methodically, new days slide into
the places of their predecessors. When a week has passed, Ham
realizes that he can be content with this lot for at least a good
while, though it is not one he'd ever imagined for himself.

Whatever is in the food he eats at the Everetts' begins to sate
him, to give him the weight of stone. It's not quite enough to pull
loose from him the need to know what has become of Miss Pearl
or to make him forget the city where he was born, whose language
he speaks and whose colors will always be triggered by the word
home. Oh, to return—but this will have to do him for now. These
many acres and the fruit they bear slake him, these days of wide
horizon, and it's nice to be provided them.

Some days, when he is waiting steadfastly for one of Ellis's
debtors to come around, he takes his lunch with some of the
workers on the property. Sometimes it is a sandwich he's gotten
up early to fix for himself and carried in a grocery bag, bologna
stuck with two squirts of mustard between white bread. Sometimes, like over the course of the three days he had to keep returning to the first farm he'd visited in the interests of Grover and
Company, he's invited to have a share of the beans someone has
brought. He manages to be understood by smiling and pointing,
which is a relief from trying to form words of his own, and he lets
his ears be washed over by the strange sounds that he doesn't yet
know to identify as Quechua mingled with loosely hinged Spanish: stories of highest comedy set in the parochial past, tales of

the wild things seen and noted since they'd left the scope of home to wander the lands of people among whom they could creep, utterly disregarded and invisible; memories of and longings for the people they have loved, the earth they have loved. Ham in silent accordance with the pathos in whatever it is they're saying commits, within himself, to learning their speech, which is so alive he can hardly compare it to the stilted *uno-dos-tres* that had passed completely beyond him without arousing any interest in elementary school. One day he hopes to bust out with a soliloquy of his own among them, like one of those children who sits until age four or five studying the words of his elders and is thought to be a poor dumb mute until at once, years later than his peers had started stumbling through their baby talk, he begins speaking in whole and perfect sentences. I could lend him the language.

Ham doesn't mind at all when he finds himself lost on the way back to the Everetts one day; it was only midafternoon when he left the soybean farm, finally victorious after having returned to it for days, so he has some hours of sun before him under which to course the low red hills. His car curves with the terrain, passing a tired old building only occasionally, in the very passive search of a road he can turn down that will lead him somewhere recognizable. A blush creeps into the sky domed over Ham's swatch of earth from its bottom edges, the place where the fabric of the firmament drapes over the earth.

His attention wanders far away from his hands and their grip on the steering wheel. His absentness doesn't support the quest to find his way back to dinner and bed, but it does allow him to travel even farther than this, west across two state lines and a bit south to his hometown, where—content as he is to be tiny as a flea on the great rural expanse of this part of the world—he tends to wish he was. The hour approaches dinnertime, and, if only he could find a rusty gas station on his way, a bag of chips would be just enough to settle the bitter churning waters of his stomach, but adrift as he is in past and home—these two, past and home, are becoming the same—he wishes he could snack right about now on some *graine a voler*; these were the tasty salted seeds of a white floating flower whose anchor was deep in river mud, a plant that the conquerors, many years before he was born, searching for an old-world analogue, had christened a lotus.

Making his way back toward his own body so that he can steer the car around a pothole in Alabama just in time, the envoy of Ham's mind passes a site on the outskirts of his hometown that I see much differently than he does. Jarred by the particular heaviness that draws me there, I can't help but to see it midway between Ham's era and my own, and in that spot I witness one long-past moment: a ritual barbeque of revenge. I am arrested, watching as a captured Spanish prisoner twirled on a spit like a stuck pig. All the juices were drawn out of him by the flames beneath his body, the crackling skin oozing an oil that sizzled on its drip into the fire while seasoned fighters and the head of their council looked on grimly. The body was to be carried into the swamp by the two young soldiers who had taken the life from it and laid there with a somber farewell.

Word of this would reach the Spanish camped around their own fire a few miles away, and their Creek spy—a nervous widower whose deeply pocked face marked him as the only survivor

of the epidemic that had wiped his home village off the map before it could be put on the map to begin with—would insist that
not all the land's people were like this, that this strange group
were called Atakapa by their neighbors, a word that marked them
literally as Eaters of Men. The name would become definitive, and
it would become handy in fueling the rumors of cannibalism by
which some further slaughter of the continent's people, by even
the good Papists among the foreign invaders, was justified.

How could poor unschooled eaters of the Son of Man know
quite what to believe?

7. In which dread appears

The clock within Deborah ticks. Ham plays the game of guessing which people know the living secret her body keeps, a game in which she seems to have enlisted his participation without telling him all the rules. He runs a kind of mental checklist: Bo, no; Ellis, almost certainly; Arthur, who visits every night to diffuse any heaviness that may have its hold over the air, making sure that no one in his family has taken his or her worries too seriously that day—probably not, but who could tell what he really did know beneath the rumble of that laugh? What about the many women in whose lathered hair Deborah buries her hands over the kitchen sink in a week? The men and boys whose scalps she shapes?

The planet's gravity has taken a nice, good hold on Ham; he is shedding, little by little, the practice of testing its tether. By

the grace of god, and by my vicarious assumption of the steering, he has so far avoided flipping his borrowed patched-together
little car in a ditch way out somewhere. And in the meantime,
he has learned further things about how to hold himself: how
to be so that people will beg of you and how to show them no
mercy, things he has been practicing quite naturally on Deborah
all along. There was even satisfaction in the way he could get the
owner or administrator of a farm to grovel a bit before him. He
could do it more or less by standing his ground, empowered by the
role Ellis vested in him. I walk him sometimes when he falters,
giving him the confidence he needs to continue.

He even has a running roster of untried short Spanish phrases,
and it won't be long—he's quick, it's a fact, no matter what any
teacher has ever told him—before he will know enough to be able
to craft ways to stick his toe into a conversation and withdraw
with a knowing nod or an amused face appropriate to the context,
without betraying that the rapid pace of the unfamiliar words
in response to him has actually exceeded his ability to follow in
understanding.

The terrain is almost becoming fixed in his mind, the plots
of red land with persistent shoots of grass marking them as cultivated starting to become familiar. The ranch-style houses that
greet him when he enters Deborah's neighborhood at the end of
the day, with their hedges in stages of overgrowth and the wilt-
ing periwinkle along their gravel driveways, tell him he's getting
closer to a resting place, if he dares not call it a home.

But the life Ham has now, the life that's settling into place
around him, does feel like it was made for someone else, borrowed

and slightly ill-fitting. Crowded in a house that is not too large with three others, the task of averting his gaze to avoid having to interact with anyone exhausts him daily. Whether Bo, Ellis, and Deborah take it for shyness or cowardice or simply take it to be a quirk discovered in the personality of someone they are still coming to know, Ham wishes he couldn't afford to concern himself with. He tries to deflect their judgments of him, but it's true that there are spaces within him where their real and imagined judgments are at home and grow wild, sometimes intruding on his quiet moments, like when he's driving the borrowed car between farms through vast expanses of patterned fields or standing in the early morning light when the only sound is the hard cereal hitting his bowl musically as he prepares his breakfast. He knows at these times, all throughout his being, that he is despised and unwanted, at best tolerated, in all the ways that count and not loved in any of the ways that matter. Ellis had cast him a reason to get up in the morning at a particular time with somewhere to be on most days. If it's true that a season in a person's life is marked by the particular routines that constrain its days—it has been true for him— then this time is beginning to shape and define itself as something made for someone Ham wasn't yet and maybe never would be, by the way he is chained to the hours worked for Ellis, chained to Deborah by the way she looks at him with such wanting and such need and such expectation.

The mornings, after he has freed himself from Deborah's narrow bed and the pastel pink walls of the bedroom she hasn't redecorated since middle school and gone down the little hallway to the kitchen in his undershirt and basketball shorts, are the moments he has most to his own. He brews a pot of strong coffee, pouring heaping spoonfuls on the filter, and drinks the whole thing black, pouring cup after cup for himself at the table and setting it on one of the paper doilies the Everetts use. Comforted as always by the bitter liquid, the taste of coffee one of the few constants he can count on in a world prone to sudden shifts, a binding force through time that ties him together. And there have been mornings where he's been able to gather himself, looking out the kitchen window to the small deck of graying wood where he can see the Everetts' outdoor grill perched and he can watch the rising sun glorify the heads of the dandelions that rise from their plot of backyard, and when I feel the jolt of caffeine electrify Ham's sinews on these mornings I'm not sure he'll be entirely mine to command until it wears off. But sometimes the dreams are hard to shake. And on those difficult mornings sitting at the kitchen table, he'll be paralyzed as the recall of where he's wandered in sleep flashes before his eyes. I could jump into him and save him from those visions. But I want him to remember.

So the residue of his dreams coats him like a film in his first days of working for Ellis, the images tangible and inescapable. He sees Deborah as he'd first seen her the day they met, her eyes as wild with fear as the wind was wild outside the bar where they'd taken shelter, and in this dream this street had already filled with water and become a river that debris floated in. Deborah's gaze traps him. It's the first thing he'd become conscious of when he woke up into the dream, and the second thing he'd become aware of was being on the edge of a decision, whether to stay put in the city or to evacuate like the mayor had said everyone should do. And the third thing was the rustle of plastic beneath his bottom because he found that instead of a barstool he was sitting on a giant mound of groceries, plastic bags packed with heads of cabbage and packages of lunch meat and sacks of beans, more food than was reasonable even for him to hunker into place with to ride out a storm. Sitting at the Everetts' table now, desperately hoping the increasing buildup of caffeine in his system will blast the dream from his bloodstream, he'll remember that he had indeed gone to make groceries on that day, his last in the city, and risked it all and went out into the sickly gray light of the storm clouds over the land. But if he can recall, he never made it to the grocery store, only to the one bar open, still with the girl from out of town he'd found wandering lost in the street, the girl who wore an immaculate purple velour tracksuit, her nails painted to match. Deborah sat on a barstool and cast worried glances now and then at the Midori sour she'd ordered only for the melting ice and the water sweating off the glass to mark the passage of time, not to drink or even touch, and as the wet circle spread around the glass on the bar it was true that they moved closer and closer to total catastrophe. And in these dreams that paralyze Ham of having his breakfast in Alabama she says those words, words uttered in the high-voltage frenzy he always hears when he thinks of Deborah—sometimes she says them in the middle of the street as he passes, sometimes she says them in a store when their eyes lock after he's bent to pick up an item she has dropped—"I got to get out of here."

The words had made the decision for him, that he was to flee. "Me too" is what he'd said to her in the dream as he had on the day itself, except the words were nearly drowned out by the sound of the crinkling plastic bags beneath him. And he'd said, "What's your name, are you from here?"—the preliminaries—and confirmed that she was in from out of town, as was clear as day. And stepping off his pile of groceries and she stepping off her barstool next to him, they'd held hands, pushed out the door, and hailed a canoe under the stars, for it had now become night, and they'd held each other against winds that rearranged even the shapes of the constellations ahead of them, winds that consumed all of heaven. In this dream the boat had carried them to a shore that was the Everetts' front yard, where the water stopped and became a well-trimmed lawn and the dog howled a welcome from within the walls of the family's home.

They begin to come at him night after night in his first weeks of the job, visions where his journey away from his hometown with Deborah was iterated over and over with slight variations. By the time he reaches the door of the borrowed car one morning, he's still unable to escape the dream where they didn't travel by canoe to Morrisville but entered the car of the fourth person they'd flagged down after walking what seemed like miles through the city—seemed like walking down a corridor that had been tunneled through the water or being in the center of a tunnel of wind, though it was only to the end of the block and back that they'd walked in between ducking back into the bar, surrendered to the fact that they were and would remain dripping wet—a grandmother and public school teacher who drove a Honda and accepted them into her back seat with torn cushions that exposed yellow foam through the tears in the fake leather. This part jibes with what memory tells Ham is true, and Ham remembers the intimacy the moment had forced on all of them, sitting in the back seat with Deborah, who'd offered to let him ride out the storm at her family's house, knowing he was bound to her in such a way that words were not needed between them, which meant they had barely spoken to each other in the brief time they'd been acquainted. But in a dream he can't get free of that paralyzes him on the gravel driveway with his hand on the car door, the landscape had caught fire and they were surrounded by flames, and the woman whose name escapes him told them not to worry because the rains would soon come. The rains never came in the dream and the flames rose higher in walls to either side of them, growing to touch across the road and enclose the car, and instead of being delivered safely to the bus station in Mobile—as they had been on that real day by this Good Samaritan, who only apologized for not being able to take them farther, explaining this was far enough out of the way for her—the flames enclosed them and the car grew hot. The car was permeated by the smell of the peppermint its owner was sucking on and breathing all over the enclosed space and it became warmer than an oven.

Ham has no escape for a while, trapped between the uncomfortable life of duty to the Everetts he lives by day and the dreams that pull him nightly into terror he'd thought was past, that make new terrors with which to entrap him. Everywhere he goes there's a hole to sink into. Shaken loose by the dreams of his last day in the city and exodus out, memories of that week he'd spent at the Everetts' after leaving town with Deborah fall upon him too. Visions of days he'd hoped to shove deep down within himself prevent him from engaging in conversation with the workers over lunch when he joins them, mutes their lively speech around him. Day and night give Ham visions where he can read the minds of each of the members of Deborah's family and they stand in a row in the living room to welcome him, projecting thoughts about how pathetic and bedraggled he is right through his body, making him sick. Volunteering to do housework had made him feel useful when he first came to the Everetts. But he was once held captive by a dream of scrubbing the whole kitchen floor with a rag where nothing else happened, except the strong bile in the back of his throat, the sensation he'd had during the first few days after his arrival at the house. Though he'd been reluctant to reciprocate her attraction to him, he soon found he could pour his fear into Deborah, maybe in ways that had never been possible before because there had never been quite so much fear. The distinct fear of those days lingers when he wakes up in the morning these first weeks on the job Ellis has given him, a fear that has melted his insides and turned his outsides to stone. One thing it teaches him is clear: he's walled in, with nowhere to turn.

Once, before he turns out the light on both himself and Deborah, while he sits on the bed with his feet planted in the carpet, it occurs to Ham to turn his neck to where she rests and say, "You know I have your family's car all day, most every day. I could drive back home—or anywhere, just drive and drive."

"You could, Ham," she says, her hands folded and resting on the round of her. "But you don't. All that we could do, we don't, that's the thing."

And one day Ham receives a message from Mayfly. He's not strongly attached to the habit of using the computer in the corner of the living room. In fact, the machine is not particularly fussed over by anyone who lives in the house, though Arthur is prone to use it as quick reference when he comes over, checking something on the internet to prove an emphatic, animated point he's making to Bo. He'll jump up from the wooden chair next to the screen, stamping his feet in a dance of victory upon proving beyond dispute that yes, a particular sports team did indeed win a critical championship game twenty years ago.

About once weekly, on occasions in the evening when

it seems the best route of evasion from Deborah's attention, Ham finds himself in that chair and, while the dog pads over to rest his snout on the top of his thigh, runs his few well-trodden circuits around the internet—the websites of memory, so to say. This is how he learns that Mayfly plans to make her way back to his hometown. She wants to know how it's going there, she's trying to get down for Carnival, has he been able to pick up and go on with things okay, is the town broken and crazy?

And the feeling seizes him again that he has somehow wandered into somebody else's destiny. He's been in the wrong place all along, hasn't he? Struck with sudden shame for the life of the past weeks—the shining rolling distance of his days and the warmly lit crowded nights in the Everetts' home—he sends her the briefest message back: things are fine here, life goes on in the city and he's springing back too, and it will be great to see her when she comes.

In the next room Ham's muddy high-top sneakers stand alertly beside the kitchen welcome mat, and beyond that back door Ellis is teaching his stepniece Glorie to ride a bicycle. She is six years old, tall for her age, the seven plaits on her head fuzzed after a hard day's play. Her exuberant squeals at discovering what her body is capable of—that with the metal vehicle beneath her and god's laws around her, her legs can propel her into a glide fast enough to skim the earth—reach Ham mockingly.

Mocking not only Ham's attempt at a lie but the lie that the attempt is founded on. Because he is only pretending, and

not very well, if he claims that it is only at the mercy of circum-
stances he can't control that he has ended up out here at Deborah's house—if he claims at this safe distance that he hadn't
lived with a feeling of impending doom for at least a year before
he was forced from his hometown. That doom sat like a weight
on his chest in the morning, daring him to rise. It was a ma-
ture form of something that had been building in him even as
a child, perhaps beginning on the day he couldn't have known
was the last he'd ever see his mother and that had yielded his
one enduring murky memory of her—a laughing mouth, plum-
dark lips that framed pretty front teeth with a gap between
them.

That year he lived by himself in a tidy apartment whose walls
he had painted red one night—opened all the windows and, by
means of the single spinning ceiling fan that strobed the warm
indoor light, lured jungle-smelling wild night air into the single
room where he slept and did but a little living. He laid down a
tarp he'd taken home from work and, wearing a pair of swim
shorts, rolled the red paint in two even coats on the walls. That
year he reported every day to the docks, came home smelling like
fish. There were no lovers and few companions. He was content to
let me take hold of him, to ease his loneliness.

A week or so before he was to be expelled from town, a
week before he would first meet Deborah, he ran into Wally
again after many years. He was dumping the bucket of water
he'd used to handwash some undershirts out of his second-floor
window, and the slop of the water onto the sidewalk narrowly
missed Wally's shoes. Wally, who he would soon learn had just

moved into a house around the corner with four of his friends, had cried up at him, furious and waving, before realizing who he was looking at. "Well what'd you do that for?" he ended up saying between laughs, and Ham came down to apologize and the two ended up going to get daiquiris a few blocks away, a place Wally knew where they were made especially strong and sweet, pushed over the wooden ledge to customers who had a choice of either standing or sitting on the two or three high wobbly stools whose motion had scuffed black scars into the linoleum floor. Ham's daiquiri was pink, watermelon or strawberry, and Wally's white.

"You know how much Ma would love to see you? You should come around sometime," said Wally, who had grown into the kind of man who wilted women, and Ham saw the same heavy dread he'd been living with all year at the bottom of his plastic cup.

This dread was always there that year to remind him something awful was going to happen to him. Even I couldn't shield him from it. He laid out his rooms for it so it would be welcome, this something terrible: look to the sky and it was coming, stand there and it would slam into him. There was a great abyss waiting to swallow him; think to the future and it was there, great and gulping. And he couldn't be sure that it wasn't from this great gaping source within him that all chaos broke loose in the form of the hurricane and swallowed the city.

Bo had looked into his own future at Ham's age and seen the same thing. So if he had been the type inclined to say so, and if

Ham had been the type inclined to hear it, he would have assured Ham that it got better. Or at the very least, it stayed steady.

He comes now into the living room where Ham is just heaving himself up from the chair at the desk and watches the young man curiously but not unkindly, sizing him up to see if a rumor he'd heard from an untrustworthy source fit—a rumor that not only was a surreptitious grandchild of his sealed in membranes within his only daughter but that Ham was the aimless young culprit who had planted it there. Bo speaks not a word and he and Ham each rearrange their faces to conceal what's beneath when in only a moment they are turned to face each other.

"You can use it if you want now," Ham says, having achieved an expression of nonchalance, thinking it's the computer Bo's after, not him.

Bo has been, in some essential way, as Ham is now; their two lives are closer than either would estimate and drawing closer by blood. By the time he'd reached the half-century mark eight years ago, Bo had passed beyond the limits of the life span he would have projected for himself when he was young—or that would have been projected for him—had lived longer than any of those he knew as men while he himself was a boy. He had gone flinging himself into every war they had ready for him and returned across oceans unscathed, perhaps because the horror of the battlefield was as familiar to him as the horror he'd been hardened against in his earliest years—the whispered specter that hung in the voices of ordinary grown people, who knew that they could be murdered for any public display of human dignity. His invincibility was a shock to him. At times when he let it, it took him completely aback to still be around.

Though three-fourths of his own children still live not more than ten miles from where Bo had grown up, a few fundamental details had shifted their world much further from his than Ham's had. Because death really did wait around every corner for the unsuspecting of Bo's times—whether in the guise of the disease that had killed his mother, against which nowadays even the smallest babies are protected by the tickle of a needle; or in the guise of the mob that had dragged his uncle to a river and drowned him for the offense of holding another man's gaze and refusing to address him as *sir*; or in the guise of the hunger that had sucked at his young cousin until finally the light was drained from his eyes. Bo was satisfied marrying at the age his oldest son Ellis would claim his high school diploma, pausing to choose from the buffet of paths spread before him, settling eventually on a two-year degree and some business school. When his youngest, Reed, had gone to finish up the war Bo had left half-done twenty years before under that distant sun so hot its rays scorched all life on impact, he had done it to see what further honor he could bring Bo. Whereas Bo had thought quite rightly that staying alive long enough to have kids of his own was ample homage to his father and had first gone to fight—having only just married a girl with bones so small a thunderclap might snap her or strong gust of wind might blow her away—in order to dare fate to grant him even that.

Other men his age Ham had known back home had killed or been killed by one another in dim light on rain-slick asphalt;

many were already out of their minds barely ten years past the age of reason; some were cooped up in jails they would leave as old men, or as corpses. Ham himself didn't understand how he'd escaped any of these fates he had seen better men succumb to—he did tend to go out of his mind but always came back—but he had known something was coming for him, that was for sure. It must be remembered that for Ham the sky finally did gather one day, as he'd always expected. The land heaved up and drew all its breath to blast him away. Surprising as all inevitable things are when at last they go ahead and drop out of their dread-gathered clouds and onto the world below.

"I hear you talk a game of spades," Bo says now to Ham, and the effort of forming these words absorbs the facial traces of his prior wonder and suspicion.

Ham grins, his sheepishness poorly concealing his real pride in his skill at cards. "No need to talk. My game does the talking."

The night has not yet fallen but is on its slow tumble down. The two men in the living room are horizontally striped with the late light that peeks through the blinds at the window, the red tones in Ham's face set to glowing in bars, Bo glowing dimmer with the sunlight to his back, while the pine-paneled walls of the room are made plaid, their vertical beams crossed by lines of light at right angles.

"That so? We'll see then, son, we'll see," Bo says.

He enlists Ham's help in clearing off the kitchen table. For Ham, I take the fruit bowl rolling with tangerines, the salt and pepper shakers, and the half-full bottle of hot sauce from it, and Bo wipes the wood with a damp dishcloth.

Ellis and little Glorie have left the backyard and are taking turns wheeling the bicycle back down the long block lined with tall grasses to her house, where Ellis will leave Glorie and ask after her stepfather Arthur. Unusually for the hour, Arthur hasn't yet come by, and he is due at his brother's table. In the distance, behind the row of split-level houses, low hills undulate, grass speckled with unruly purple flowers and the hazy forms of grazing cows. Glorie dreams of being able to travel as far as her eye can see with her bicycle, to the limits of her known world.

Deborah, meanwhile, clicks through the aisles of a dusty grocery store two miles away in high heels that once belonged to her mother, Azalea, beneath the spasm of the store's fluorescent lighting and between rows of bright pickle jars and jellies, her red plastic shopping basket on an arm. She knows the sting of vinegar will satisfy her tastes, suspects she could guzzle it straight but has considered that eating relish from the jar would accomplish the same thing with somewhat more decorum. She already has bananas for Ellis in her basket and a few sticks of sugarcane for Ham. This yearning for vinegar with all her might is surely from beyond her, a command from the tiny new captain of her body.

All that Deborah knows, she might have said just as aptly to Ham the night before, she doesn't tell. Her particular power is drawn from knowing what she knows, not from telling it. And in knowing what others cannot say, their unformed needs. This power is the assured control with which she nods her head when she is passed in the aisles of the supermarket by people whose hair she styles, or by others who have known her in any number of capacities since she was a child, as when her elementary school teacher Miss Gladys, now retired, passes pushing a basket filled with baby formula for her grandchild and reports that the family is doing well and that, though her bones creak, god is good all the time.

Oh, it's true: something would rise up inside Deborah and threaten to rebel now and then, against the life her mother had left her with, this life lived attentive to the needs of men. But then Ham had come, and he needed care. She is relieved that a creature that now has needs that are clearly not her needs grows inside her. Relieved mostly, but resentful too—maybe now she'll never get to know who she is outside of her service to others, maybe it's too late for that. Already.

When, having paid for her things and having sat in the car in the parking lot in front of the supermarket slurping relish from the cold glass lip of the jar until the jar was half-empty and having made her way finally home, Deborah walks through the door, Ham, Ellis, and Bo are posed around the table expectantly. They turn their heads toward the sound of the door like eager school-children waiting for a word of instruction. Arthur, laid up down the block with a flu in its earliest stages, will not be joining them. It is Deborah who, after placing her plastic grocery bags on the counter and removing one by one the items therein to put them in their proper places, takes the seat opposite Bo, a gesture that marks her as his partner in cards. It is Deborah who cuts the deck neatly after Ham, the dealer, has shuffled and who slides the deck back to him at her right.

When Ellis first shoots a glance at Ham, his partner in the game, after having assessed his own hand, it is to tell Ham, wordlessly, not to mess things up for them. He is soon to learn that the card game of spades is one undertaking at which Ham is almost always successful. And it's not because he has me over his shoulder—I don't guide his hand, I don't supply him with premonitions of what cards the other players will lay. He has the instinct in his own fingers. He has not placed much importance on this skill or bothered to find out what else it can be applied to, but it is a certain fallow satisfaction of his.

There is minimal trash-talking during this game. If Arthur had been sitting in Deborah's place, the kitchen would by now be raucous with his challenges, instigations, cries of victory and defeat, and with some of the same from Ellis; Arthur has the power to draw just a touch of rowdiness from his ordinarily solemn brother. As it is, between his initial mistrust of Ham as a competent partner and his chivalrous regard for Deborah's delicate ears and the barely formed ears of the one within her who hears everything, who knows nothing, but whose body will be molded by and imprinted with whatever stirs in the world around it, Ellis is on his best behavior. He hasn't much to say as Ham neatly cleans up the opposing team, comprised of Bo and Deborah. Though Deborah is a formidable player and leads her team to win the first few rounds, Ham patiently and effectively—with only a smile, at most a thoughtful "hmm"—catches up and passes them in points, leading with what he has been dealt when his cards are high or using his lesser cards to support Ellis's better hand.

"That's how it's done, folks," Ellis says as, pleased, he gathers all the cards and rises when he and Ham have garnered a high enough score to conclude the game as its winners.

8. In which all three waters are applied

Deborah's parents had divorced when she was in high school. Bo was still helplessly in love with Azalea, Deborah's mother. For more than a year after the divorce she had lived in the basement of the same house, drinking too much. Her depression had been an ongoing thing. She waited until she could hear no motion from the floorboards upstairs before coming upstairs at night to eat alone, sometimes cooking meals at midnight to leave for Bo and her children to eat during the day, until she became an unspoken-of thing, a secret hidden in plain view. Deborah recalled the smells and faint sounds of cooking that reached her in the middle of the night at that time, figures in the darkness, the longing to rise from her bed and go to her mother and the force that always squashed that longing. Sometimes even now Deborah pretended she was still down in the basement, in hiding. In reality, Azalea had escaped to Florida, where she had newly committed herself to clean living and worked as a fitness instructor for the elderly. For the first months she was down there, a couple years ago, she had sent Deborah a postcard every week, always postmarked on a Tuesday, a picture of a different beach, sand and sky and ocean lit in sunset or sunrise or high noon. Some canned message scrawled across the other side: *Wish you were here*, or something like it. Deborah kept these postcards in her bottom drawer with a rubber band around them, where they remain to this day. Now Azalea calls once a month. If no one is home, she tries back until she catches Ellis or Deborah. Bo never picks up the phone if the caller ID shows an out-of-state area code. But he gets reports, not from Ellis but from Deborah, usually brief:

"Mama called, she's doing good."

"That's great, Peaches. Tell your mother I love her."

He never fails to ask that this message be conveyed to his ex-wife. It is never conveyed.

Ham wants to make his break too, seeing exits everywhere, mind filled with possibilities of the best way, the best moment, to leave. He schemes even while watching Deborah in the kitchen, dreams of escape while resting his head in the crook between her shoulder and neck. Knowing that this kitchen is not his real life, and just as sure that a real life waits for him if he can only catch up to it. I can't stop him from dreaming of escape, though I might want to. Ham's dreams, at least, are his own.

The plant Deborah is cooking, pokeweed, had been gathered by Bo earlier that day. He'd rooted through their backyard, and, with the kind permission of its elderly proprietors, the backyard next door. He had taken pains to part the grass softly with his bare dry hands in order to identify the right plant, a low-growing thing, its leaves sheltering the shameless bright red of its stem and its small black berries. Bo had plucked enough of the leaf to fill a small canvas bag he wore slung to his side, from which he'd drawn a bottle of water now and then to quench his thirst. He has promised his neighbors their share of the poke salad that he knows Deborah will be glad to make from it.

This plant Bo has gathered, whose leaves Deborah found beginning to softly wilt within the sack that had been placed on the kitchen table, is deadly poisonous. If eaten raw it kills quickly. But if it is prepared with great precision, by some strange alchemy its poison abates and it can be transformed into a simple, savory dish. Deborah had learned the method by spending several years of her childhood in fastidious, discreet guard at the side of her mother, Azalea, who, after years of disregarding Deborah there, finally tugged her daughter by the shoulder one day and said, "You watch, you pay attention to this. One misstep and you poison the whole family."

"You cook the plant in three waters"—this is what Deborah is explaining to Ham, who looks on. "First boil it for about ten minutes. Throw out the water. Fill with fresh water, boil again. Throw out the water, cook a third time, now adding a sliver of fatback to the water. Separately, fry thinly sliced onions in oil, with a little garlic and green pepper. Add this to the pot with salt and black pepper."

Deborah woke with a strong taste for it, though poke salad has not been prepared in the house for years. That morning she had found a ladybug, lost and wandering across the vast reflective plain of the kitchen counter, pinched it between her fingers, and felt its last desperate movements buzz into her teeth as they crushed it. She had told no one of these strange habits she had fallen in thrall of: imagining her growing child a spider, a predator, a creature spun of its own cunning. So she had no one to tell that eating the ladybug had not served to squash an urge, as she'd hoped, but to spring a further urge out of her. And had caused her to feel that she could never be at rest until she'd eaten some pokeweed.

Now the scent of the greens begins not only to fill the house but to hint to any who pass by—while it is cooking those passing by the Everetts' place include a cat in heat who yowls with blind desire and the mailman, who cranes his head when the scent reaches him.

Within the house, in the next room over from his kitchen and its rising smell of poke cooking, a yearning swells in Bo as the scent reaches his nostrils for times when nothing could be wasted. His appetites were formed by and still crave food cooked in sacramental remembrance of days when every part of the pig, like the meager strip of lard that imparts the last of its taste to the poke, was saved and savored and sucked-over—when by some miracle and with enough grease and flour a meal for six could be created from little else. When the little, barest scraps of green clinging to the earth, gathered and divided, multiplied like the loaves and fishes. Tasting this dish that has been wrought by his daughter's own hands will return him to times he remembers, to times he doesn't have to remember, and to times so long ago he couldn't possibly remember. To longed-for horrors, the terror sweeter than mother's milk. To the devil he knew then, away from these strange new ones.

And, lured, who will show up at the threshold to partake of the meal but Arthur. He could not have smelled it cooking from his house. Who knows what he is responding to when, on impulse, after two days of resting sick in bed, he jolts upright to fling water he hasn't even bothered to let heat over his back in the shower. To fasten his shirt—a shirt Deborah had pressed with Bo's and Ellis's and now Ham's laundry—all the way to the top button. Perhaps the sacrament of the meal has called to his blood in some other way.

He hurries. Gingerly steps over Glorie, lying on her belly in the living room putting together a jigsaw puzzle. Quickly bids goodbye to his wife despite her insistence that he take it easy and hustles himself down the long block until he does smell it: greens from the yard flavored by pork cooking in a tall pot sending the aroma out in every direction like a lighthouse sends its beams.

He arrives, pushes through the unlocked door. His glance passes over Bo on the sofa, who cannot see past the haze of his reverie to notice that his son has just entered the house and greet him. Arthur looks over Bo to the small dining room, where he sees the polished oak table set the same way it had been the last time he'd eaten the meal whose scent now calls him from tantalizingly close by. The table is laid with a simple set of porcelain plates that his parents had received as wedding gifts. The porcelain set has long been incomplete, and the plate at the head of the table has been replaced by a cheap plastic one from a different set. Arthur himself had broken the original long ago on his first day of school. Six plates are laid out now, despite the unlikelihood that all the table's places will be filled at dinner.

"Why y'all eating in the dining room? Special occasion?" Arthur calls to Bo. There is no answer from his father. Arthur is left with no shelter from himself but the distorted reverberations of his own voice against the chinaware. To quickly fill the silence, he taps out a beat against a plate with his fingernails before he is saved from stillness by a cough that wracks his whole body. He draws up his arm to cover his mouth with the crook of his elbow, but only after spraying a few tiny droplets onto the clean plate before him.

"You don't sound so good, Arthur. That's why I told you to stay put," Deborah says from the kitchen over the low simmer of the pot. She hadn't recently told him any such thing, but she would have, and she would have expected her advice to go unheeded, so it was as good now as if she had said the words before.

Arthur, opening his nostrils and allowing them to fill with the smell of poke, sees the table's seats filled by his family, sees them as they had been when last they'd eaten the meal those remaining were about to enjoy now: poke salad, navy beans, store-bought potato rolls, and leftover chicken from the refrigerator, ready to be microwaved right before they sit down. He takes the seat he would have taken then, and for a minute he sees in the chair beside him a young Ellis, with that little teenage mustache he wore that could be mistaken for some ash or soot he had gotten smudged above his mouth. He sees across from them a young Deborah, and he blinks back the metallic flash of her braces as she parts her lips to smile uneasily, shy in her own home. He sees at the head of the table Bo, whose face, hair, and style of dress have not changed since. He sees his mother, Azalea, at the table's foot, thoughtfully resting her chin in cupped hands, her eyes on him and her ears on his words.

During that meal long ago, Azalea alone had enjoyed Arthur's tirade about the latest incident at football practice. She hoped her son could pull her, with the force of breath behind his words, securely onto his side of the dark chasm that stretched before her, so that she no longer felt that she dangled over its ledge. The others paid him no mind, wanting the flavors in their mouths to be undisturbed by their outside attentions. Still, Arthur spoke as though he was fighting to be heard over a racket, as though his claims that the quarterback had tripped over a rock in the field rather than Arthur's foot were being loudly contested by Deborah and Ellis and Bo, coming at him from all sides with their objections.

But this time it will be Ham who ladles the greens onto Arthur's plate so that he is finally engulfed in the cloud of their aroma. And it will be Ham who takes it upon himself to rouse Bo from his armchair and to call Ellis, at work at the desk in his bedroom. It will even be Ham who pulls out the seat beside Arthur for Deborah as she approaches the table, eager to rest her feet and eager to taste (tasting will help the child within her remember what world it's coming to).

Arthur blesses the food before them. Tasting the tang of the poke, Ham feels the vine of this family's blood curl tighter around him, entangling him ever further. I take my own seat at the foot of the table, opposite from Bo, the place reserved for ghosts.

III.

WHAT IS REDEEMED

1. In which Ham takes flight

Ham is convinced that every one of the Everetts can see through him to his point of utmost vulnerability. Deborah had spotted it lying raw within him on the day of the storm, the day they first met, and it was what she glimpsed forever after when she would turn the corners of her mouth down at him, too polite to ever accuse outright but having a martyr's sense of suffering him, of bearing his weight. Ellis and Arthur and Bo marked it in him right away.

Then there was this new reason for whatever suspicions they'd had about his weakness to be confirmed. Deborah, terrified, had called 911 late in the evening, and he'd been taken in an ambulance to the hospital, barely breathing. Wherever the condition of asthma had come from, it was clear that it had chosen Ham for its own. Though Deborah might have wanted to blame herself for having fed him the pokeweed, thinking maybe that had set it off, she was composed enough to know better—after all, the poison would have killed him outright. Ham stayed two nights in the hospital and was sent back to the Everetts with an aerosol inhaler in every color and a prescription for some pills and a long list of instructions, which Deborah had written down on a receipt and neatly tucked into her wallet so that it could be accessed for reference before bed or first thing in the morning.

It feels like being in debt, which he also was now: owing his continued existence to a chemical regimen. It feels like being an electrical appliance whose life would vanish if its plug was yanked from the socket, this paying rent on the air he breathes. He tries not to think about it. It gives me more time to do with Ham what I will.

Bo and Deborah take him to eat at Ezekiel's Valley of Dry Bones the afternoon he leaves behind the atmosphere of the hospital and its unnatural combination of staleness and sterility. Ezekiel had inherited the Valley of Dry Bones from its founder, his father Ezekiel.

He had made no alterations to his father's original menu. There was still only one thing on it: a rack of ribs, accompanied by bread and butter, served with one side dish that alternated on a weekly schedule. Potato salad Monday, Wednesday, and Friday, coleslaw Tuesday and Thursday. On Saturday the side was candied sweet potatoes and on Sunday slabs of baked macaroni were served. The barbeque sauce Zeke used on the ribs was a family secret. It had been passed to the founder of the restaurant by his own grandmother. The current Zeke carried it all on.

Deborah had worked at Ezekiel's one summer in high school, had once worn the same T-shirt and apron as their waitress does now when she brings out steaming pork ribs heaped like a glistening, ill-constructed hut and a pile of thick slices of buttered bread.

Ham is surprised to sight his friend from the farm, Gomez, through the cut-out window that looks into the kitchen, wearing unsoiled white and chopping onions with utter diligence even as his eyes well up. Gomez doesn't see him. In this setting, Ham is cloaked with the invisibility of the unexpected.

It is two days before Fat Tuesday, and at the table Bo announces his intention to give up pork this year until Easter. These weeks have crawled out of Ordinary Time and onward to approach Lent. This means that Ham's plan to be home in time to seem as though he'd never left—was it a plan, really?—looks grim.

Perhaps Mayfly is there already, back in his hometown. Yes, he sees her, short-haired and breezy, filling cracks in the city's decay with herself. Sees her walking down streets where he'd lived, drunk on bourbon and glee, leaning on a good friend for support, singing loud songs up to streetlamps, cries that rise to become part of the swelling voice of the city, its one voice jubilant and triumphant, sated enough with the pleasures of the flesh to withstand the meager forty days and forty nights to follow.

As asleep in the hospital bed, Ham had wandered.

And upon returning he felt that old pull: the feeling I've

come to know, myself, as being sucked into the body of another. Sweet gravity again. Snapped into place, you wiggle the fingers, as though it's a glove you're trying on, not a hand itself. You blink in adjustment to the view from new eyes.

This body was Ham's own. This body, its motions converted to electric impulses blinking on the monitors beside his hospital bed. Its rhythms simplified so that doctors can measure it as a fine, ticking machine.

Once he had awoken, he'd had an underwater feeling. He felt a salty film on his skin as though he'd emerged from the cool dark oblivion of the ocean and drawn his first open breath. Waking, he'd felt shipwrecked against the day.

In the coming week he starts to recall things. These recollections sneak up on him in patches: shivers of what feel like memories, but from no life he's lived.

For instance, setting a bowl of water on the kitchen floor for the dog, he'll be seized by the vision of a street in Lima, stretching uphill ahead of him like a gilded river, shining and wet from a recent rain. His bare feet on the kitchen linoleum flexed with the muscle memory of having gripped slick cobblestones, in sandals worn so smooth that any protection they might once have offered from the elements had become symbolic. He can see everything glistening as he made his way to a patient whose leg had been crushed by a wheel—the kitchen in Alabama seeming to glisten as the street had with those wet trees draping their dew-jeweled branches over every wall alongside him.

The doctors had given him one prescription, along with instructions that he wean himself off it when it had done its work, in tight half-measures. So he was to take four pills a day for four days, then two on the fifth day, then one on the sixth day; then use a knife from the kitchen to cut one pill in half and, swallowing that, be done. It's easy for me to walk Ham in his weakened state, so I do.

The day after he had swallowed that last one-half of a pill, I have Ham agree to take Gomez to work for his second shift at Ezekiel's. I can use the words in his head to shape his familiar tongue and teeth to convey whatever intention I like. He meets Gomez around 3:30 in the afternoon, the sun lazily poised in the last quarter of its sky. I animate his legs to pad at the earth with a quick pace as he makes his way to meet his friend, but the anticipation in the heart is Ham's.

As Ham and Gomez return across the field, three or four crows caw to one another, pecking at wasted grain in the field. In his mind Ham floats above, flooded by memories of being everywhere at once, of being scattered on the wind in particles—of being the wind itself. Soaring, he can see for miles.

He hears someone's voice. Then he realizes it's his own voice speaking, saying to Gomez, "This car is mine."

The two of them enter Ham's borrowed car. Gomez in the passenger seat clicks a cassette tape into the player: a woman's voice, warbling like a bird and on the edge of weeping, fills the car.

"Just one more week here," Gomez tells Ham. "And then Texas."

They arrive at Ezekiel's, where the waitress—Irene, a friend of Deborah's—is spreading checked picnic cloths on the wooden benches out front. Ham and Gomez go around to the back, pushing the door into a kitchen shining with aluminum fixtures, a bareness and the fresh-blood smell of cold meat, barely masked by chlorine. In a porcelain sink on the wall, Gomez scrubs his hands free of soil until black rivers run down the bowl.

Ham has never been in the habit of revealing himself but somehow winds up telling Gomez about how he'd found Deborah just the day before; he'd looked out the back kitchen window to find her on tiptoe outside, removing the cover from the light above the stoop. She had not been aware of being watched through the blinds, but Ham saw her. And he saw her dump the plastic cover of the porchlight over her cupped palm, and he saw the ash-like particles that poured from it dance in the air above her palm as they settle into a mound of fine dust, a dust made of insect wings.

"I saw her," he tells Gomez, "eating bugs."

Gomez looks at Ham, incredulous, not sure if this is some slip of the tongue, some failed attempt to grasp a different word choice.

"Bugs? Like the things that crawl on the ground? With six legs?"

Ham swears it.

Gomez shakes his head before tying a bandana around it and slipping his arms into a white smock. Ham follows him into the restaurant's dining room, where they take two pint glasses and fill them with one of the beers on tap.

"Take me with you"—and at first Ham feels like he's joking. He speaks seldom enough that his words to Gomez, when they come, seem to hold the weight of rare, significant wisdom.

Gomez laughs, so maybe it really is a joke.

Drinking, they survey the empty Valley of Dry Bones. Everything is in its place, chairs neatly upended and stacked on the tables against the wall. On the swept wooden floor the vague bright reflections of the furniture are cast, and in the silence Ham is reminded of an empty church or temple. Everything clean and next to godliness.

Irene enters, swaying. She sets her broom down, then visits every table to turn the small plastic vase on each one upright.

They watch her switch around the room. Finding the scissors in a pocket of her apron, she goes out again for a few minutes and returns with a bundle of daises clenched in her fist. She places a stem in each little vase so that on every table appears the tiny upturned face of a flower, each looking for a sun that can no longer be found, each sufficing to settle its little gaze on one of the restaurant's hanging lamps.

Irene moves to stand beside the bar, her arms folded, her frown pensive. After she has decided that she is pleased with her work, she turns to Ham and Gomez.

"What are you two scheming? And give me a little of that," she says, taking Ham's glass and looking him square in the eye, daringly, as she sips from it.

"Nothing," Ham says, and then Irene laughs because he sounds so guilty, and he has to laugh too.

"I got schemes too," Irene says. She hasn't given Ham his glass back yet. "One of these days I'll probably own this joint."

"Is your name Ezekiel?" Ham asks her.

"This one has jokes!" Irene says. And finishing Ham's beer, "But I know all about you. Things you don't even know about yourself."

Ham feels something unsettle in him, but he presses anyway. "Like what?"

"You won't be long around here, I know that much."

"Maybe you do know something I don't then."

That's when Gomez turns to him and says something like, *You're young, there's no sense feeling like anyone's prisoner.*

So Ham admits, "But then maybe I've been thinking about that too."

"We could always use one more."

"It's honestly not my business," Irene says, shrugging her shoulders and relieving herself of the matter. The way some people coquettishly eye the truth, peeking at it and then shying away.

Then Zeke's footfall reaches their ears at the bar. A distant shuffle that serves as the tolling of a bell: hurry to your places, the ship sets sail.

Ham nods to Irene wordlessly, as though bowing beneath the brim of an invisible hat and then turning his face to the light again. He pats Gomez on the back. He gathers himself off the barstool and jingles his key ring to accompany the tune he's begun to whistle, tosses the keys glinting into the air as he leaves the Valley of Dry Bones.

From then on, the days are a countdown. These days are taking on the weight and the beauty of last days for Ham.

One day, picking up the car down the block at Arthur's, Ham squats on the floor with Glorie to play dolls with her. Glorie is the master of this domain, sets the rules and enforces them. The one family of dolls is preparing for a volleyball match against the other family of dolls. Ham is asked to help change their clothes—the one doll with the dirty face whose blond plastic hair has all matted up into one big ball, and the other—this one's eldest daughter, whose head has been squashed halfway down its neck, after Glorie had accidentally decapitated it one day, breaking the head off its pivot in what was explained to the other dolls as a bicycle accident.

The painted lotus-feet of the dolls are made only for wearing high-heeled shoes, but the sharp plastic shoes they'd all come with had long since snapped off, never to be seen again until one stabbed into the sole of Arthur's bare foot, causing him to chuck the tack-like thing against the wall in pain. Glorie asks Ham to supply the voices for the one male doll, which she uses to represent two different people.

Ham knows he has no good reason to run from this halfway belonging among Deborah's family. Halfway is better than no way at all. There's a future in halfway.

But he is starting to have reason to believe that when one world has sealed safely behind you—when you step away—you could view it as a world among many worlds. That you could feel yourself growing at once too large for one world and too, too small against everything yet to be known.

He is starting to believe in the power of leaving.

It doesn't take long to stuff everything he owns into his backpack, and so Ham takes the time to get one long, undisturbed look at

Deborah as she sleeps and considers what's growing in the mound of her belly that lifts the covers. The eyes behind her closed eyelids flutter wildly to trace the shape of strange dreams.

Ham lets sadness find him. Not because he'll miss her, but maybe because he won't. Maybe he mourns a little, knowing he can never find that thing in her she clutches for so desperately in him.

Under his gaze Deborah stirs, and her own eyes find themselves open, not knowing whether they are still dreaming.

Ham pulls himself together to say, "I'm leaving, Deb."

I want to jerk him back, have him take back the words, make him stay. I'd rather he take root here, be subject to all the expectations they have on him here and more susceptible to me. He's cornered here, the easier for me to slip into him, and I fear what lies ahead if he breaks free of this place, whether I'll be able to take hold of him. But I restrain myself. This decision has to be Ham's own.

Deborah rises up onto her elbows. She looks at him, but she does not see him. She sees past him.

When Ham had left her the first time, Deborah could not wrest her mind free of him—god, how she tried—but she could not pry the phantom of him off her. She'd crawl into a far corner of her bed to sleep, expectant of him when she opened her eyes.

Dragged in circles, reliving the memory of him, she created a map of each time he'd touched her. She could remember the smallest downward gesture of his glance, sitting beside her on the bus home, if some small tenderness lurked. If she had to draw the connecting lines herself, all the points were there. Enough pieces to know that she was loved.

The evidence was all clearly catalogued. September tenth, he gives her his slice of toast at breakfast, leaving no bread for himself. September fourteenth, he opens the door for her when she taps on it from the outside with an elbow, her arms full of groceries. The way he touched her arm on the bus home that long, long night: like no other arm had ever touched an arm.

He will always be lit up in deep blue for her, the color of bruised twilight the storm had washed them with that early morning when they crossed out of the city—crossed it to cross it again who knew when. If they survived: if the wind didn't follow them everywhere, didn't keep whisking them up as easily as if they had been two dust bunnies blown into a corner to be devoured. To wait for it.

Deborah feels that the crossing alone should have bound them. And that a new life came out of it, something in which to throw all the dead hopes of the last one: that had to be more than enough.

"You just got out of the hospital. You're sick, Ham," she says, swallowing. "You can't go."

"It'll be better if I do. I can make more money if I go, for the baby. I'd be doing more than just earning my keep."

"And come back?"

"I'll come back."

"You won't come back." Deborah's face full of snot and trying by all means to hold back tears.

"I will. I will come back, and when I do I'll bring enough to give."

Right outside, at the end of the drive, the truck purrs in waiting, with Gomez and the others inside. Ham opens the front door into that same blue color, that same time of day when Deborah first looked at Ham next to her and knew that into this man's hands she would commit her spirit.

The chaos of the storm had been any and all things to those caught in it, but for Deborah, for all its sudden violence, it was also the benevolent force that had introduced Ham into her life. When she'd gotten isolated from her friends that day, caught in the midst of rain and howling wind under the Jax sign, it had been Ham who had blown in on the current and rescued her, knowingly shepherded her into the bar where they'd ducked for cover and eventually helped hail the ride that took her back home and away from that drowning city that would become just one small unfortunate blip on the surface of her memories, receding into the past. Now the one she couldn't help but see as her rescuer was leaving her to fend for herself. Hearing the truck take Ham away, Deborah pulls the blanket to steel herself for what she may have to face alone.

2. In which new worlds roll by

In the back of the truck Ham pretends to sleep. He recalls being a child in homes where the voices of grown folks floated over him at night. He is swaddled by the knowledge that this next day will be like none he's ever seen before, and he's washed with the murmur of strange voices: quiet, early morning talk among the others, and a song that Gomez begins to harmonize with a fellow from his hometown. They pass a lake of water only a little while away from Deborah's house. Ham begins to travel backward in time, to when he left high school in the middle of his senior year. An older man named Charley, whom he'd met in a bar, invited him into his house encircled by white verandas. He stayed there a few months, pretending he didn't know that some mornings Charley stood in the doorway of the room where he let Ham sleep, just looking at him for an hour or so.

Ham began to make his way, apart from the earth—barely touching it with his feet when he walked. There had been a few months after his nineteenth birthday when he had tried to get into the habit of drinking himself to oblivion. It didn't work; he was always still there. So he gave it up and waited to be taken up by the wind and carried out of that world.

It was happening again. He was being carried away.

The truck cuts through the rising morning. Four sit in the front cabin: Diego, the driver, a man in his forties with a thick gray mustache; two men on the middle seat, the brothers Hector and Juan; and Pablo at the open passenger's window tapping a cigarette out into the whistling breeze.

And four in the back: Ham, curled against his backpack; Gomez and Absalon and Lucas. Someone passes a thermos full of black coffee through the back window, and in ceremonious turns, each one in the back takes a swig. The coffee is lukewarm but potent and pries Ham's eyes awake. So this is what it is like, to lift like birds from off the land. Buoyed by the wind. I feel through Ham's senses what it's like, the rush of the wind and the cramped spaces in the back.

They are headed through Mississippi. Pablo up front has a cousin who lives near Natchez, whose home they are aiming for in time for nightfall. They'll spend one night there, then set out in the morning to make it close to Fort Worth, Texas, by the following night.

Trees tumble past now, spooling the day open. The others in

the back look at him and smile when they see that Ham is alert and among them. He considers them each, catching for a brief moment the shadowed eye of Absalon, the youngest of them, whose baseball cap is pulled low over his brow. Absalon is here because that was what boys did when they became men in his town, went north to find their fortunes. He was blown about amicably, here and there, led by forces he trusted.

Lucas has been talking about his father back home, who needs a new heart. Over the course of two years Lucas has saved half as much as he needs. Piecemeal, he hopes to be able to patch his father together again, like some Humpty Dumpty. Somewhere out there, beating in the chest of some stranger in Brazil, is the heart that is marked for his father.

Lucas paints the picture of his father pining for a heart in that backwater Bolivian town, a homeplace everyone present knows well, except Ham. Every day, grandchildren, Lucas's nieces and nephews, enter his parents' house to kiss his father's liver-spotted cheek. Some of the little ones fear him—his smell of death and his squinting eyes, his mumbled frog-croak speech that only other grown-ups can understand. But they are made to kiss him. They are made to show him their paintings from school, as though he will bless them from his bed. The strong man Lucas knew, who had lifted him on his shoulders as a kid and carried him, was a stranger to these young ones.

Yes, Lucas's father will have his heart. Lucas will be sure of it. A secondhand heart, wrung free of the fears and hopes of its original owner, to learn a new beat.

Around midday Gomez breaks out a deck of cards. For the

first time since he's been hanging around them, Ham is invited to be not just a spectator of the game but a player, one of the anchors of the imaginary table's four corners.

Gomez has been working all this time toward the dream of a wife. He has the whole setup nicely laid out in his imagination: the house he will build for her, the children he will fill her with. After he deals the cards Gomez passes around a photograph he carries in his wallet of one of the two contenders from back home, narrowed down from the field of eligible young ladies in his town and the next. It's a school portrait of a sweet seventeen-year-old, a few years younger than him, whose mother is a friend of his mother and whom he's patiently watched grow into womanhood. The girl grins in pigtails. The other girl he's considering, Gomez explains, is the nice-enough-looking daughter of a family of some means in town, whose storefront business he could stand to inherit if he plays the good son-in-law well enough. Whichever girl it turns out to be, Gomez wants to have the perfect place for her to fit. The works.

They take only one stop on the journey. It's around noon, and they are in some Mississippi town that seems to be entirely covered in tangled kudzu, so that it seems like some timeless mythic village where people live among the vines, peeking out at the strangers in curiosity from behind their veils of green. There is a vine-overgrown convenience store, and Diego fills the gas tank while the others wander indoors to the restroom, except for Ham and Gomez, who see no problem with unzipping in the field behind the building, watching their twin arcs of pee sparkle in the blinding afternoon sun.

Then back on the road. Diego drives at a very even pace, never pushing too far above the speed limit. They cannot risk being stopped by the highway patrol. Ham, with his tattered ID, is the most officially documented among them, bearing more proof of his right to be on the road than even the vehicle itself.

Just as the sun dips out of sight, they arrive at the home of Juan's cousin. Juan shouts their arrival into the air. Shutting the doors to the truck, the travelers are pulled by some unseen force toward the beckoning open door of the home, from which the laughter of children and the smell of corn drift out. Indoors they find the table spread for them, and each helps himself to a tall glass of ice water.

The morning of the day he'd left the Everetts, he'd been in the kitchen at the counter making a sandwich for his sack lunch, patting a slice of bologna atop a smooth spread of mayonnaise on a piece of bread, when Ellis had come up behind him, swift and silent in socked feet, and gently placed a hand on Ham's shoulder. This time Ham had been quick enough to glance over his shoulder to see the larger man coming in enough time to throw out a "good morning" before turning back to his task, but not in enough time to keep Ellis from reaching out a hand.

"Hey," Ham had said, trying not to sound startled.

"Things are good?" Ellis asked.

"Um, yeah, they're good."

"With the position, I mean. Rick told me he likes what he sees, says accounts that haven't paid up in ages are sending in checks."

"I guess so. I mean, that's good."

"Maybe it's not a bad thing, having you around."

Ham was wary of what he perceived as tenderness in Ellis's face. It might be a trick of the early light. Now, sitting around the table to a simple meal with good company, he pushed away the idea that he had started to belong in the Everetts' home. He's where he's supposed to be now, going wherever. He washes the memory down his throat with a huge gulp of ice-cold water.

Having eaten his fill, Ham finds sleep for the night in an armchair in the living room. In the twilight, before drifting into a dream, he sees the laughing face of Christ, and in his mouth hangs the taste of the Eucharist dissolving on the tongue.

3. In which Ham is granted visions of Miss Pearl

Finally, in his dreams that night, he meets Miss Pearl. And he knows that it is her, though she is diminished. It's not so much that she's aged but passed through age to its other side.

He wants to touch the smooth round of her cheek. But he's afraid that if he does reach for her, she won't be there. So rather than take her hand in his, or take her small body into his arms, he looks at her. Holds her gaze well. And she smiles and begins to speak, but her voice is muted, as if it's gurgling up from underwater.

Maybe she means to assure him that while the water rushed into her home to claim what was its own, she slept. She did not even stir when the waters rose to the top of her bed and began to gently lap at the hairs on her arm as she dreamed a final dream in which a newborn puppy licked her bare skin. Eyes closed, she let the water cover her eyelids while everything was washed clean, baptized. While everything was washed away.

The water slithered in under the front and back doors, rising up and into the shotgun house. The walnut tree that grew in the yard of her neighbors across the street, people she'd played with when they were children, was lifted by the wind, carried on the water, and guided through her living room window, breaking the glass with no more force than you'd use to crack an egg. Pierced, the house let water enter its wounds from every direction.

Miss Pearl was carried out of her home through the window; her mattress became a raft. A goldfish, someone's pet, swam between the curlers that began to loosen from her hair as she drifted. The street became a canal. She floated with objects sacred and profane: water-stained family photographs that had been on someone's mantel, and flowers that had been uprooted from where they grew, and beads that had draped trees, and cigarette butts, and swirling ash. Were they carried by the sea, or had they all become the sea together?

I know, Ham says to her, I know.

And did I ride the wind or had I become the wind?

What had months before been a sea breeze contained in a dusty bowl of the African desert eventually gathered enough heat to become seaworthy again and to twirl like a furious pinwheel over the Atlantic Ocean. The storm's churning is patient, its mounting fury insistent. The ocean feeds itself into the mouth of the storm, the winds assume water. The mass of it, the wind and water whipped, led by the Gulf Stream into the warm waters of the Caribbean.

Then I see with the compassionless eye of the hurricane its motion gathered around a center of calm. When it collides with the land it discharges its force into so many shattered objects—lives, some of them. Then it, too, becomes nothing.

Why should the storm pity what it destroys? When it is destruction destroying itself? It will be born again, then dance itself out. And it doesn't matter what you call it on its countless returns—whether you give it any name from A to Z, or a number, or try to measure its miles from side to side. Only its turning matters: because it turns like the stars turn, like the earth turns, like the wheel of time.

He doesn't engage with the others much on the journey the next day, turning inward to sights he hasn't laid eyes on in a while. He'd recently acquired a cell phone from working collections for Ellis, and he'd woken to a missed call from Deborah. He didn't have any minutes, somewhat fortuitously, so he couldn't call her back just yet.

The vision of Miss Pearl settles in him with the weight of new knowledge. He can recognize the fingers of sadness anywhere, and he is not surprised to feel their grip on him now. He doesn't fault himself for this irrational feeling of loss: a feeling of loss for what you never did have, and for what you cannot be sure is gone. He just lets it overcome him, watching the dry palmettos that now line the highway beg for mercy from the sun. Smiling with big sad eyes when someone in the truck cracks a joke and the others laugh.

When they stop for gas across the Texas state border he buys a card for his phone and calls Deborah while the others stretch their legs. He is taken aback at the sound of her voice when she answers.

"Hello? Ham? Can you hear me?"

How strange it still is that someone can be reduced like that to just a voice in the darkness, just a voice miles away, just a voice you can hear as your eyes set upon vistas the one you speak to can't even imagine.

He likes her better this way. He can't say it. He would never be able to convey the tenderness he feels. The whole picture of her is in her voice. From that distance, the voice is naked, the intimacy of voice into ear closer than anything.

"Can you hear me?" Deborah says. "Listen good."

"I can hear you."

"It's going to be a girl, and her name's going to be Margaret. Margaret May, okay?"

"Okay," Ham says.

"That's what the doctor said, that it's going to be a girl."

"Margaret May." The words light on him like the name of a stranger a seer has told him he'll meet one day. He asks, "How's everybody doing?"

"Oh, they're fine. Mad."

"And you?"

"Me, I'm alright. Because I always knew what you are, Ham. I always knew."

"Well, what am I?"

"You're like the wind, Ham."

Unfazed, he hangs up, mumbling something restrained, then wanders back over to the waiting truck. Diego asks him, "You alright, man?"

He's okay.

He is one of a herd now, and he likes this. He feels borne up in a mass migration, moved like a fallen leaf floating down a stream. Before climbing back into the flatbed he asks Pablo to share his cigarette, and they sit tapping tiny balls of ash onto the white plastic table outside the gas station store, watching the wind play gently with the ash, rolling it to and fro.

They keep riding. Vistas shift, and though Ham notices the people in the cars they pass—people behind glass, looking faded by the sun—no one seems to throw a glance their truck's way. For much of the day's ride everyone in the truck is asleep but Ham and Diego, and the two yell to each other now and then over the roar of the breeze through the window.

Feeling his chest seize again—the sensation he is coming to anticipate and to fear—he fumbles through his backpack beside him, finds his inhaler, and, removing its cap, takes two frantic puffs, while Diego's eye stays fixed on his in the rearview mirror.

"My son has asthma too," Diego tells him.

"I don't, really, it's just for now," Ham assures Diego. This is when it dawns on him that when he has run out of medicine—if he pushes it he can stretch it out for about two months maybe— there is no more. And that after that he might be in jeopardy.

"Yeah, I'm supposed to be over it in about two months," Ham tells Diego. Realizing that he has no choice but to get over it.

"With my eldest, it was very bad," Diego tells him. "He had

to spend a week in the hospital when he was young. He was supposed to be the ring bearer in my brother's wedding at that time. He was so sad to miss it.

"But it will be alright, man," he tells Ham.

Other than the eighteen-wheelers they run alongside now and then, most of the other cars at this hour seem to be driven by people on their way to work: sleepy uniformed or polo-shirted people. Ham sees one woman lazily focused on her driving. Her bony bare feet pressing the car's pedals are beneath Ham's view and he cannot see the ugly high-heeled pumps resting on the passenger seat beside her.

Parents are among these drivers too, their kids slapping one another in the back seat. Farther and farther behind Ham fades the familiar. They are all in it together, all these drivers and their passengers.

Diego calls out his sighting of an armadillo, a waddling little tank of a rodent making its way down the shoulder of the road. This is the first time Ham's seen an armadillo outside of television. It's a different country out here.

If he could describe what the air was doing—what it seemed to be revealing of itself as it reeled Ham farther west than he'd ever been before—it would be a paling, a shift to pastels, though the color they'd started out with in the vicinity of Deborah's house had been deep and dark, the trees lush and sturdy.

In the group he's traveling with, Ham has begun to take his turn, as they each do, as lookout. Looking is something he does well anyway, and now he at least has something useful to do with his alertness to danger. He has also noticed himself falling into the role of interpreter more often than not, as when the parking attendant at a rest stop tried to hassle them, or when the man behind the counter at that convenience store near Natchez had tried to charge Absalon double for a candy bar.

Back at Deborah's house, miles farther and farther away, it was true what she'd said to Ham: things were fine. "I told you so, Deb," Arthur says to her in the kitchen, pressing into her shoulder with his heavy hand in what was meant as a touch of comfort. Ellis doesn't say much but one night he does assure her, without meeting her eye while moths fling themselves at the windowpane from outside, making percussive pings as their bodies meet the glass, "We'll get through this, Deborah."

Ellis, the family's only churchgoing member, had just returned from Mass. There, in his linen sports coat, he had gripped the lacquered black wood of the pew in front of him to steady himself as he swayed with the others in his row, singing:

Take me to the water
Take me to the water
Take me to the water
To be baptized

None but the righteous
None but the righteous

None but the righteous
Shall be baptized

The frankincense that filled the room lifted Ellis's prayers up to god. The same prayers as usual: for justice and for deliverance from evil.

Bo says nothing, but standing in the front yard smoking a cigarillo he fantasizes about wringing Ham's neck. Sending his smoke signal out, the tiny beam of the cigarillo's cherry like a human lighthouse, it occurs to him that he might have done exactly the same thing. Supposing things had been different for him and he'd been stupid enough to get himself into the same kind of mess as Ham.

In all these months he and his daughter Deborah have not once had a conversation about the advancement of her belly or what she might possibly be keeping in there. Neither one of them would have known how to approach such a conversation. And anyway, what can words do about it? The thing itself is bad enough.

Deborah, meanwhile, has been dreaming since Ham's departure of standing in the rain. Sometimes it's a rainstorm accompanied by the static crackle of lightning and dark brooding clouds. Other times it's just a sprinkle. Always each point of water hits the top of her head distinctly, and always at the end of the dream she realizes that each of the million droplets falling from the sky and impacting her body is a tiny insect.

She does not have the images to picture Ham as anything other than absent. He is like the proverbial tree falling in the depths of a forest far, far, far from where she can hear it crash to the earth.

While far away from her knowing, the truck that carries him away hurtles down the highway. The truck arrives at its final destination at last in the middle of the night, in the deepest dark, in a land where silence presses over everything with palpable weight. There is not even a thin wash of the moon here, just the pinpricks of distant stars. Everything is veiled under the cover of night. So that when he and the others shuffle into the one room where they will all sleep for the next few weeks, Ham does not know what in the world he will be waking up to. Surprise me, he tells the Lord.

4. In which Ham finds himself in another country

The blinding Texas heat soon seizes all Ham's senses.

Diego deposits them all in the middle of a cotton field. They have taken a detour, Ham learned from Gomez. Diego had heard of this opportunity and couldn't pass it up; they would head to pick pecans afterward. Gomez shrugs when he tells Ham, ambivalent. With an authority gleaned from his days with Grover and Company and nowhere else, Ham finds the owner of the property and marches up to the house of graying wood where he lives with his family.

"Ain't it supposed to be a machine that does all this?" Ham asks.

"I'm old-fashioned, I guess. The picker broke, still have the gin, though. It'll be back in a few weeks. You want to go lollygagging back to wherever it is you came from, I don't care, there's plenty more who will do the work. But if you want to make a little cash here you'll do as you're told."

Ham, city boy, did. He looks around him, bewildered by the pretty white bolls and the scorching blue expanse of sky. He puts his hands on his head. He turns, embracing the strange fate he has chosen.

The work is fraught with hazard: hacking off as big a portion of the plant as he can while avoiding being pricked by the daggers that surround him in the plant's thorns, placing them in the sack strapped to him, from where he will feed them into a machine that separates the cotton from the chaff. Ham soon learns to avoid the barbs. But within only a few hours, he is ground down by the endless repetition. At noon, the choking heat of the sun slams into the earth all at once: like clockwork, Ham thinks, like the working of the original clock. At first I can do the work for Ham, using his limbs as though they were mine, but as Ham heaves and hacks he starts to resist, to take hold of his own reins.

In two days they are all several shades darker than they'd been before. This land has given them a new skin, a costume. Ham and Gomez always work side by side. They speak little, but sometimes Gomez will whistle and leave gaps in the tune for Ham to fill in—so Ham finds himself humming into the spaces, surprised to hear the sound of his own voice, the clear timbre of it.

They soon learn where they can drink in the closest town, just twenty minutes away in Diego's truck, but Ham finds himself pushing away a glass of beer more often than not, comforted enough by the people around him and even by the way his body aches, signaling to him that it's done what a body was made for.

Ham lets the heat all around him consume him—a heat he comes to learn does not disappear at night but is only disguised by the darkness, cloaked in humidity. The heat becomes his only reality. He lets the heat make him new, lets it put a fever in him. At the end of the first week they all stand in a long line to receive their pay from the supervisor, a tall man shifting a giant wad of snuff back and forth in his cheek, the skin at the back of his neck thick as an elephant's and red as Georgia clay. The supervisor counts them each three hundred dollars in cash for the week, one by one. Ham holds the fifteen twenty-dollar bills tight in his fist, then he folds each bill neatly and places them all in a compartment of his backpack, patting the new bulge in the pocket with his hand before zipping it tight. It is not a lot of money, all things considered, but it's worth it. He thinks of it as Margaret May's money. He has people in faraway places now. That's become a part of how he lives—with the ghosts of those he has loved, or not quite, or who have not quite loved him back hanging over him. It's nice because he is never alone, always in a crowd, the crowd's only bodied member.

But you were never alone, Ham. Don't you know you always had me?

It is now that I begin to know who really holds the tethers between us, and who can snap them at will. The others enclose around him, his friends. He becomes one of them, having never really been one of any number before. His unloved empty spaces are becoming filled. Soon I will be crowded out. I try to grip Ham, to seize him wholly, but he resists.

After a month here Ham's other lives have become one distant dream tinted rosily by nostalgia.

So it no longer matters if he never fell into a family by birth, or that he was never chosen by a group of other boys at school, or that he has spent the majority of this past year trying to earn the belonging of a girl who could never know how to love him and her family that could not even try.

It doesn't even matter that no one in his varied childhood had thought him particular enough to photograph him at play or in someone's home, so that he does not even know what that boy he had been looked like.

Here he could let the sun bleed it all out of him; here he was made in the sun's own image, smoldering as the sun, shining as the sun.

So things go for the better part of a month. Solace, sun, soil, and the most wrenching bone weariness at the end of the day that ferries him into rock-solid dreamless sleep at the end of the night, and the spider legs of dawn reaching toward him in the morning, pulling him awake effortlessly, and the cold water stinging his face as he washes it, and the sun again, dirt again, the bite of cotton barb, a streak of blood, the touch of a finger on his arm and the black crescent of dirt under those fingernails that match his own, and the salt-gritted taste of ridged fingerprints on his tongue, and a stroke of heat over the afternoon.

He thinks to call someone—to report that all is well here with him into a listening ear. He wants to see if he can mark some change in himself in another person's sight. And he wants to imagine that someone is wondering about him and might be glad to hear from him.

Naturally Mayfly comes to mind. After all, she surely understands how it feels to be set loose, to let the unknown cradle you. It occurs to him that Mayfly is also one of the few people, if not the only one, he could try to get in touch with right now. There is almost no one he could call at this stage who would remember him, care about him, be interested in him, hear him out, or some alchemical mixture of all of these. He doesn't count Deborah.

To move his digestion along, Ham takes a long walk after dinner, and he brings his cell phone, into which Mayfly's is one of the few numbers he's programmed. Underneath tall ashen trees he dials her.

In her home in Atlanta, on the other end of the miles-long invisible signal that connects them, Mayfly's phone, resting on her sofa—the very one on which Ham had made his home some months ago—makes its pulsing electronic scream. The parakeet in the kitchen responds to it with words of comfort in its own language.

Mayfly—a time zone away from her caller, an hour forward into the sun—is out. Whipping through an Atlanta alleyway on her bicycle, she recognizes a tug in her thoughts toward Ham. Mind that she hadn't asked Ham to enter her life, ever, and not now either. She harbored some bit of nostalgic affection for him for sure but wanted nothing to do with a longing, nothing that pulled or weighed.

So that as he enters her mind now, cutting into the concentration she'd been channeling into pushing the pedals of the bike, she wonders what could possibly be significant about him. It bothers her to feel she has a need for anyone. It bothers her to be disturbed by someone's memory. She has long since severed allegiance to anyone else, family included. This feels something like that, an allegiance.

Standing on her porch in bare feet one morning to check the letterbox that was nailed next to her door, Mayfly had met her neighbor Marguerite, who occupied the other half of their duplex. Marguerite was getting her mail, too, wearing a nightcap over her hair in curlers that pressed themselves against the cloth so that their exact raised shapes were outlined.

"Morning, love," she said to Mayfly. "Say, whatever happened to your—was that your brother or something?"

"My friend. He went home."

"Oh. Don't you miss him, all alone here?"

"I'm fine."

"That's right," Marguerite said, "I know you are. You'll always be just fine."

Mayfly hadn't thought of those days, that time in her life—that younger, foolish self she had split out of like a moth from its cocoon—in years, not before Ham sent her a message and then literally showed up on her doorstep, bringing the past with him in great engulfing clouds.

But even after he'd left, it was still with her. Standing on this side of herself, looking across the chasm Ham had bridged to things that had been. Those days had imposed themselves on these.

Soon enough Mayfly had started hearing reports from people she had known. Kids were moving into Ham's hometown, attracted by its rot. She had one old friend who was setting up an amateur, illegal tattoo parlor off of Rampart. She was planning on starting a new tattoo, an eagle. She wanted its wings spread across her back.

They were moving into neighborhoods whose life they stood apart from. This was something she knew, not something she'd been told. When she got there—hopping her first train in years—she saw for herself that it was as she'd expected. She hadn't found Ham anywhere. She hadn't bothered to find Miss Pearl's house.

When she walked in the company of her old friend Patch, there were no nods to those they passed on the streets. There was no joining the birthday cookout they passed in someone's yard, no dancing to the bounce music that blared from it, no submission of requests or a favorite song.

She didn't know which side she was on anymore.

My own side, she decided as she rode back, by herself. My own damn side.

She arrived back in Atlanta just in time to get fired from the call center for taking a leave for that week to travel. She saw it as having a definite bright side. That script she'd had to read to solicit money from the hostile and the indifferent; the rage of strangers; the boredom; the blast of the air conditioner that required her to wear a sweater indoors in July: all were behind her now.

So she collected unemployment for a month until she found a job, through a friend of a friend, as a bike messenger. It was great: weaving in and out of traffic, the constant whip of air on her face, so that she could pretend, while riding, that the wind was her only master. So far she had avoided injury. She put aside enough to get the eagle on her back filled in a little more every month by an artist she knew there in Atlanta. It was beginning to look alive, like one day it might choose to lift itself up from her skin just to feel the breeze fill each hollow of its feathers.

Ham, nervous boy, sullen young man—whichever he was—should have vanished a long time ago, into the mist where other charming people she had briefly known had faded. He should have taken his bow as the curtains on the stage of her memory closed around him.

But there he had been again, the ghost, right on her own front porch. Heaven knew she herself had needed refuge before, so she didn't mind offering some to anyone who did not arouse her suspicion.

Standing there in the light of dusk, having wandered a few blocks through her neighborhood until he found her address, this grown version of a little boy her mind had long ago left in its recesses had a hunted look to him, like he had narrowly escaped some sort of fanged predator. He seemed for an instant to remind her of skins she had shed.

"How old are you now, Ham?" she had asked him after inviting him in, and when he told her she saw herself as she'd been at that age, not as long ago as she usually liked to think. She too had been coming to Atlanta then, to beg at its door, and had thought herself world-weary, hardened by the elements.

No, she didn't at all mind sheltering this specter, not at all, for as long as he needed. But she did not want to touch him, or to examine him too closely. She did not want the smudge of his sorrow to rub off on her. She wanted to be unchanged by him.

And she cursed him now for still entering her mind. She

damned him to hell, to the ghettoes of the imagination, to banishment from it. What did he still want from her?

The funny little boy. Tense but trusting, and eager for mischief, as she had been then too. She liked to listen to him talk when they met—that thick drawl carried on the tiny voice. The way he let his spoken *O*s just hover on the air like smoke rings. When they exited the corner store where they had found each other to see what they could find together in the day, she lifted the hat from her own head, a blue baseball cap with a faded UNC logo, and pushed it down over Ham's head for him to wear, laughing when she saw how it slipped loosely down to shade Ham's small face.

But Mayfly had met a lot of these kinds of people, amusing-enough folk she could have a good time with who each showed her something a little new about the way the world was. There were many to whom she'd poured out whatever was in her heart, many for whom she'd been a vessel for their heart pourings, in many cities to which she knew she would never return. Sometimes she ended up learning their names, but not always. Sometimes she had cause to remember them fleetingly a month or so down the line, but usually she didn't.

"Do you ever just want to be your own whole wide world?" she had asked the bag lady she'd once stumbled on who was picking through the garbage at the end of one long country gravel drive, at a party one night where an anarcho-punk band played raucously to the moon and the flowers and butterbean stalks in the garden were drenched in beer, when she had wandered far from the assembled partygoers wild and dripping with sweat, to see if she could hear what stars sounded like out there, where they were splattered over a cloudy wash of the Milky Way.

"Look, your territory ends where mine begins, girlie," the bag lady said to her warily. "And there's other people than you in this whole wide world of yours."

"I know you're right," Mayfly told her. "But don't you want to disappear into yourself sometimes?"

"I'm already invisible, love," the woman said. "And believe me, it is the best thing you could ask for."

It's true. The joys of invisibility are precious ones. But the question Mayfly really begs of Ham now—wishing to be shaken free of him by the breeze billowing her shirt as she rides—is one I recognize. I have asked it and asked it myself, in life and after. I asked it of my creator, the beloved: how do you have your hooks in me?

It is only because I know something Mayfly doesn't that I can occasionally be satisfied with no answer. I know that we do not belong only to ourselves, that what loves us also seizes us.

5. In which pastures grow green

I know what it's like to be left behind, though not by Ham. In life, I learned to live without my father. This deliberate effort—a toning and a conditioning of my heart's pathways by the exercise of compassion, as Christ has shown us to do—gave me not only the strength but the weakness, the flex and the emptiness, to do as I was called.

My mother never objected when she saw what god had made me for. She could see the clear signs from the time I was small; how ants who made militant black lines into our home in search of the unsealed honey pot somewhere would redirect themselves, track apologetically backward, if I, as a small boy whose human speech was not yet well-formed, asked them to, and how I could rap at the house's walls to ask termites to kindly desist, let them know where they could find a rich store of wood no one needed. Like Deborah I was drawn to cutting hair and was skilled at it, but in my time this act was also bound with the medical profession. That meant I was in the right place when I apprenticed with the barber in our town as a young man to learn the many ways of cutting living flesh, of excising, and of hastening the closing over of a wound.

After the rumors had spread despite me of the things the creator could use me for, my father came looking for me. It was more than a decade after he had left my mother to pursue glories her body could never bear for him; her body, whose dark strength and beauty was drawn from the strength of the earth's fertile, rich, deeply potential soil itself.

One evening at supper in the monastery, a priest of our order with whom I had grown very close came to sit next to me at our long table made of grayed wooden planks. He told me what little he could—without breaking the sacramental trust between his confessor and the god for whom he was only a humble surrogate on the other side of a latticed wooden wall from the sinner—about a nobleman, a Spaniard with my name, who had come to him to confess and who seemed to have a particular concern for me, perhaps an interest in seeing me.

I said to Father, "Tell him to look at the profile of his own shadow, his own outlined shape, next chance the sun gives him. And he'll see me."

To which he replied, "Haven't you forgiven him, Brother?"

"Yes, and I am free of him."

I won't be abandoned again. Ham's body grows stronger, and his hold on it does too. The sun bores into him in the fields. He resists me, prefers to take hold of himself. His hands know to hack, stuff, hack, stuff. Sun, bramble so brown as to be black, then those white puffs, sky scratched up with thin cloud. This is what Ham is coming to know. After cotton country, there is melon country. The cotton picker, majestic monstrous eater of thorns, came to signal their time to pile into Diego's truck and head toward the next destination.

The fields are verdant, green melons and their vines. The air is fresh, and Ham's ownership of his body ever tighter. One Sunday in melon country Ham and Gomez take a path through the woods, down to the reservoir tucked away within them, not far from the farm but hidden worlds away from its view, through a dusty wilderness. Snakes flit between rocks ahead of them, and tiny lizards sunning themselves cock their heads at the view of the two men, before darting away on such fleet feet that they seem to have vanished into thin air.

The two wash their clothes with a bar of soap in the muddy water. They drape their clothes to dry over the branches of a tree on the bank, before slipping into the water one behind the other. The cool of the water licks Ham's skin. Gomez laughs at the water's touch and Ham laughs at Gomez's laugh. The sun's rays play on the surface of the water, and when their movement causes a splash, a bit of the sun's light is carried glinting into the air in each drop of water.

Emerging, they take up their things hanging on the tree, their warm T-shirts and jeans imbued with the fragrance of the sun. They walk back to camp down the path again, their hands swinging so close in the space between their two bodies that Ham could clasp Gomez's, if he'd wanted to. Ham doesn't want to tell Gomez just now that he's decided to go back for his baby, because there is no need to speak of a future in which they are separated. And if he did tell, it would only open the opportunity to be dissuaded. But Ham is sure in his course: he will have someone to be his own, someone to shape in his image, someone to command.

Under the sun the next day they learn, via shouts across the rows of living barbed wire, that it has not taken Diego long to find a mistress. There is a young lady in the nearby town where they go to drink that he tithes a bit of every paycheck to—for the mending of a blouse of hers, some gold-colored sterling silver earrings, a drink here and there, a bite of this or that to eat. He has budgeted for this, he assures the eggers-on, he always does. His son will still be standing in a new pair of Nikes at the start of the new school year, his wife will still be able to keep the house stocked with the roundest, ripest fruit on offer.

Ham doesn't mind the melon work, heaving the melons into a waiting truck while the others in their rows do the same. In the evenings a woman named Rosa cooks for them and the tens of others who sleep and work on the farm. Dinner is served at eight every night, and the company around the three tables in the old shed that has been converted into their mess hall is always assorted and lively.

Hector, one of the brothers they'd traveled with, reveals himself to be a sturdy, hardworking drunk once they settle into the rhythm of days in the same place. Ham has observed with admiration as Hector wakes himself with a swig first thing every morning, works all day with superhuman strength, gulping quantities of water and gin on his breaks, and drinks all through the night. He might be a willing, unwitting host for me to enter; but I'd have to stand in line behind his many demons.

They will pick melons for two months, rarely able to sneak one away, break it, and open its sweet insides to the sun.

6. In which an old friend reappears

We each move when the wind hits us according to our own natures. The chime sings. The rotting tree falls. A baby cries. A man out in the sun sighs when the breeze lifts the sweat from his skin.

The wind shivers over a jaguar stalking the forest somewhere, over the powerful lift of his shoulders as his front paws impact the ground. He is looking for a wild vine to eat that will give him visions. He heaves his great body into an acacia tree and ascends its branches, batting through the vines growing there in the way that he would hunt a rodent scrambling up the tree—playfully executing his game of high stakes, where the jaguar's victory is assured and the penalty for losing is death. He plucks a few leaves with his fangs and chews them and sucks on their cud.

Descending from the branches of the tree on light feet, the cat rolls on its back in bliss, crushing the patch of herbs growing in the wet black jungle floor and sending their fragrance into its fur. He is entering a reverie, preparing to meet the spirits of the birds he seeks as prey, to ask them to surrender their lives for his sustenance.

It is then that I slip in, now flexing the paws that have become mine, feeling my own force as the surge of breath that ripples the muscles underneath the black hide, an undulating silken sea.

I lead myself to the men who have been hunting me for weeks in vengeance for the death of a child in their village. Their party was hungry, lost, about to finally orient themselves toward home, defeated. They are at first fearful at the sight of me, then weapons are scrambled into their various arms, and they watch in puzzlement: I lay down before them in the middle of camp. And the rifle blasts a hole into my side. I exit the body with its life force and its blood.

And Ham wakes to the memory of having been an animal, with a cat's keen senses for hunting, the taste of blood in his mouth. He swears his eyes flash yellow for an instant in the mirror the unbroken water in the bucket offers when he goes to wash his face.

When Mayfly calls him back, he is on his way to the fields, under a newly risen yellow sun.

"Hello?" Ham says.

"Who's this? I got a call from this number," Mayfly's voice clear as electricity.

"It's me."

"Me who?" Mayfly asks him. "There's billions of *me*s."

"It's Ham. I just wanted to say hi."

"Ham. Ham, right? I put you up for a couple months recently, didn't I?"

"Yeah, that was me."

"And I knew you when I was younger too, didn't I?"

"Yeah. One summer."

"So are you doing fine?"

"I'm better than fine, actually."

"That's good. Me too. So what is it that you want, Ham? What do you want from me, exactly?"

"I just . . . thought I'd see how you were doing."

"I see. You need money, something like that?"

"No, I've got some of that. I guess I just—"

"You just wanted to hear my voice?"

"Maybe so."

"Isn't that sweet! Well hey, don't call me again, okay? I have nothing for you. Zero. I couldn't even remember your name until you showed up at my door that day. Get it?"

"No, I don't get it!"

"You're just going to have to figure it out on your own."

"The thing is, I know why you like to run away and leave now. I like it too. And it's okay."

Mayfly's bitter, sarcastic resolve is assaulted by the gentleness in Ham's tone.

"What do you mean?"

"I think I wanted to be you. Free as you, that is."

"We could've been each other's heroes," Mayfly relents. "I just never wanted to belong to anybody, like you never seemed to belong to anybody."

"What I wanted to ask is if you are in my town, because I'm coming back, and maybe we could meet there or something."

"I'll think about it. Why not? It's not because I owe you something or I'm attached to you."

"No, I suppose not."

Hanging up, Ham staggers onward to work where familiar faces await him. Pairs of warm brown eyes extend their greetings to him, as do the warm rays of the sun, as do the ripe melons nestled among leaves on the ground.

It's not long before he is seized by a wheeze in his chest. The inhaler in his pocket is almost empty but it will do for now. Two puffs. And what later?

He'll hitch a ride into town this evening to drink with the others. The bar will be nearly empty before the five of them arrive, just one mournful gray-haired regular slouched over the counter on his stool and a girl in her work clothes in a corner jabbing her coins into the jukebox now and then to change the song.

They bring the party with them. Ham is not quite unaccustomed to this godless feeling he has, a feeling of abandonment.

No, a feeling of freedom. He dances with the girl in work clothes, pulls her by the arm up to himself, and they jerk back and forth like two little kids playing at a waltz. They are laughing, both of them, overcome by silliness, dancing the twist and the macarena and all manner of senseless moves.

Diego is shooting dice with Pablo at a booth, and they have money on the table, and Absalon leans over Pablo's shoulder to cheer him on. And these are Ham's people for now, he thinks, casting a glance over his shoulder while his arms flail joyfully every which way. And when he wants new people, he will find some, as he always has.

He makes sure Diego has enough to drink tonight. And sliding him another cold beer he persuades him to stay just until the early morning, when the pharmacies here will be open. Then he can get a refill on the medicine he needs.

"We'll all sleep in the truck," Ham tells them at three in the morning, when everyone's good sense has long since faded and the bartender has grown tired of trying to tend to them. Diego pulls the truck around back to the dirt driveway, and like lost wanderers each of the others finds his way to it, and each tucks into his nook and surrenders to sleep.

Ham's dreams aren't much, dulled by drink, but in them I watch him stage himself as his own hero. He is absent in these dreams of any longing or confusion. There are no strangers. He does not watch anyone from the sidelines, as he most often does in dreams: observing dramas that have nothing to do with him, aware of himself only as a watcher, a pair of eyes.

"If I can shake off one ghost, why not another?" he asks when he catches me. He has cornered me in a room down some dark hallway of his imagination, where I am wearing a T-shirt of his and the room is smothered in the thick seawater scent of Ham's hometown.

Not me, Ham. It would be like cutting off your arm.

When Ham opens his eyes, dazed in the back of the truck with the others, the sky above him slightly spinning through his hangover, he moves to lift one arm to prop himself up on.

But I lift his other arm instead. Strong drink, Ham thinks, that could make a man forget how to move his own body. When Ham gathers the effort to coordinate all his limbs, I confuse their movements so that he ends up tumbling over the side of the truck bed, jolted firmly awake by a thud into the dust and gravel.

His friends are all laughing at him now.

I'm your puppeteer, Ham. And I'm the only cure you'd ever need, Ham, if you'd turn to me.

And now there is a morning gray. The town in the thin light of new day glimmers like a tub of muddy dishwater, and the truck slides through the town's three stoplights in full command of an empty road.

They all get out in front of a locally owned pharmacy with dingy windows. The others browse the cluttered shelves of the pharmacy and wander its narrow aisles, plucking the drinks and snacks and phone cards they want to buy. Ham makes a hurried beeline for the pharmacy counter at the back of the store, just as the tired-eyed and balding pharmacist is pulling up the clanky tin screen that seals the counter at night. Out of breath, Ham fishes through his pockets for the crumpled doctor's prescription that indicates he has the right to buy his medicine. He's thankful his tactic of swaying Diego to stay until morning has allowed him to make it this far; he'd had no other chance to get his prescription refilled. And I'm thankful too, for reasons beyond him. Because his mind was elsewhere, circling anxiously in anticipation of being able to get the medication his life depends on, I could jolt his steps in an even, calculated pace. Today, he needs to be in position, on his mark, at the precise time.

The pharmacist says it will take thirty minutes to process. Ham marvels at this, seeing the rows of shelves fully and alphabetically stocked with all the medicines anyone could ever need. He doesn't understand why it's going to take half an hour for the pharmacist to turn around, shuffle over a few feet, find his medicine, and pull it off the shelf.

But he has no choice other than to wait. He seats himself in a hard Formica chair. There's a contraption he can stick his whole arm into, have the blood nearly squeezed out of him by the tightening cuff encircling him in its python grip, and see his blood pressure numbers displayed as disjointed red-eyed analog digits on a screen.

The numbers don't mean anything particular to him, but they are a comfort somehow. Numbers always tell the truth, and so do machines.

The cuff sighs, exhaling the air it had pumped to grip Ham's arm. When he is free of its clutch, he stands and shakes his arm out. He finds his way blocked by the body of a stranger he hadn't seen when he was seated facing a wall.

The face of the stranger coagulates into something familiar. Something in him registers this as someone he knows, but it is not until the other man speaks in Wally's musical voice that he realizes who.

"Wally!"

"Looks like we just keep running into each other, Ham!"

"How'd you get here?"

"I could ask the same of you!"

"I'm with these guys," Ham says, gesturing at the only other customers in the store.

They stand back and look at each other, grinning. Ham's smile is bashful at first, then he breaks out and bares teeth and from his belly comes an irrepressible laugh.

"I tell you what, anything can happen, Ham. If all that's happened has happened, anything could happen. So I guess I shouldn't be surprised at anything, not even the sight of you."

"Once you break loose and surrender to chance, life has this way of sending all kinds of things. It's what I'm learning. God, it's good to see you," says Ham.

He tells Wally of this new life of his, the slipping into and out of these forgotten towns like a pack of ghosts, and the sweating under the sun, and the clarity the monotony delivers—the focus blinding in its brilliance.

And Wally? He had been set to rambling strange other worlds himself. He didn't get out of the city before the storm. He didn't try, thought he could wait it out. His mother Pearl had long taught him that they could hold out against any storm—the storm wasn't for them, she'd said. It was a cleaning of the earth, a rupture in Creation's fabric through which those whose work here was finished slipped.

Wally had stayed home alone and had taken care to close all the shutters on the outside of the house where he lived with his friends, even those that required him to get out a ladder from the shed and climb like some knight whose Rapunzel had bound her hair for the evening. He slept tight, unfazed by the chaos that lifted the old world from underneath them all by darkness, and had woken to a wasted town. So it ended up that he had found himself shuffled with thousands of others into a sports arena that had been slap-handedly converted into a mass shelter, a place that began over the course of the three days he was there to swell with the visceral odor of despair, and sweat, and sickness. An aroma reminiscent of the hold of the transatlantic slave ships that Peter Claver, born only the year after me, would board to pull souls from the stinking swamp wet with all manner of body fluids to claim them for Christ's team—a belly cramped with the born and unborn bodies of the living, dead, and dying.

"And your ma?" Ham asks Wally.

"She . . . we don't know," Wally says. He turns the corners of this thought around in his mind and flips it so its poles will line up into something he can believe.

"Oh, okay," Ham responds.

Wally tells Ham how he was able to return to the house. Before the great upheaval, Wally had been living in the same house where Ham had run into him the year before.

"You know I like to see that she's alright," Wally continues, "so I'd be over there now and then, changing a lightbulb or mowing the grass for her. I'd come over to see what her house needed every Sunday and she would fix us a little dinner. She was taking it easy though, taking her due rest, and she didn't mind asking me to bring something from the store or some takeout."

"And you didn't mind bringing it."

"Not at all, Ham, I never did mind. No. I minded her."

Wally tells how he was able to return to the house quite a bit later, by which time their neighborhood had become a swamp of sludge, crawling with spooks and elephantine insects, and he watched a dragonfly as long as his arm get snapped up in the jaws of a nutria as big as someone's dog.

It was a couple weeks before he could slog through the wet ruins of everything they'd ever known to finally make his way to the street he'd grown up on, which was not at the time recognizable as a street at all. He came to the crumpled, tilted heap that had once been his mother's house. The shape of what it had been still framed it, in spirit at least. The heap of the splintered home cocked sideways, leaning away from the sun. This was fully a month before a crew would reach this block and spray on each building an *X*, a sideways-tilted cross, a code so that crews would know what was worth saving and what wasn't.

The house would be marked by this coming crew as devoid of any living thing except the mildew whose festering blossoms bloomed across its surfaces and within its crannies.

"She was gone," Wally tells Ham, "I'm certain of that. She must have escaped to somewhere safe."

When Pearl was a girl she had slept with her head in her MeeMaw's lap at a party one night while a hurricane whipped up a frenzy outside the windows. The grown folks danced, drank bourbon, and cut pound cake for the children. Pearl's MeeMaw said that the storm could never touch them, though it came again and came again.

"Did you talk to her at all the day before?" Ham asked.

"Yeah, a little. She wasn't sure if she was leaving or staying. She didn't want to leave the cat alone."

And she was unconvinced that this thing was going to be any fiercer than the many storms she'd lived through. Remembering to him about that party, the glee with which adults and children alike had stomped the storm down, its tropical force wailing outside in frustration, unable to harm them at all, until finally all its fury was spent, the city having outfoxed it yet again.

"But you haven't heard from her since."

"No. She's out there though. She wouldn't leave me. She wouldn't leave us, Ham," Wally said before swallowing the thing that was trying to rise in his throat.

"So I was in Houston for a while with family, thinking of making my way to California."

"Why, what's out there?"

"A job I guess, and my aunt."

"Miss Pearl's sister."

"That's right, you got it."

So the wind had moved over Wally and set him into motion. I could not have commanded Wally's steps. He'd always been beyond my reach, even when he was a boy. I see him now, lit fluorescent in the aisles of the pharmacy, with the same sure posture and the same winning smile. I play in cracks left in Ham, and maybe these were sealed in Wally by his mother's love. A current beyond me had drawn Wally up to meet Ham here, taken him on his own parallel adventures into the wild chaos beyond their hometown. I couldn't have jerked Wally's limbs the way I now force Ham to scratch an itch he doesn't have, flexing in him like a hand in a glove, ready to act if he is unable to carry himself where I know we must go.

Ham blinks. Between his eyelids he begins to see Gomez approach them from a side aisle.

7. In which tongues of fire rain down on the heads

Wholly ghost, I go down singing songs of the day, singing toward sons of this time. It is a lighthearted going down. I have known these sinews well. So when Wally asks Ham what he's doing today it's easy for me to move his lips and say, "Nothing." And easy to ignore the hurt glimmer in Gomez's eye as he stands before us—a foreigner to our country, nothing else.

And it's likewise easy to walk down the middle aisle of that pharmacy and into the morning's waiting arms, into its great beyond. We can start drinking as early as we feel. The sun, the sun! It is a great winking eye high above us. Its light touches my skin, kisses freedom into it. Now with a firm hold on Ham, I ask Wally to wait just one moment as I enter the pharmacy one last time.

Diego is at the counter. He's bought a little candy dispenser

with the head of an animal from some cartoon film at the top—
you lift the animal's head and a sweet sugar pill pops out.

"For your son," I say to him.

Diego says not a word, but he smiles. In his smile I know his
only fear in the world is of being an inadequate protector of his
children and his wife.

"He'll love it," I say.

"Almost time," Diego tells me.

"I'm not coming," I say to him.

"For what reason?" he asks me.

My smile, a reflection of his own earlier one, holding against
the puzzled expression that's begun to creep into his brow. I buy
a six-pack of beer, imported ale in green glass couched behind
wet-cool cardboard.

I leave. It's what I do. It's easy, simple, and free to do so. It's
pure delight. I leave bodies. I come again. I leave them. I stay
away. And only the leaving is mine.

The door slides closed behind me on its electric beat. I'm
out on the sidewalk with Wally again. The others, who were my
friends, are penned in together in the building like cattle, far from
me. Let them herd on, less one.

"Well, what about work?" he asks me.

"What about it?" I say.

"You crazy, Ham," he says, "always been crazy."

"Touched," I tell him, to clarify.

We wander the six blocks of this godforsaken town swinging
my black plastic bag from the pharmacy between us. I lead myself
as I'd led the jaguar to its just death at the hands of its hunters.

And I walk Ham to the waiting park bench where he and Wally can hear the very sound of the sun rising, its ecstatic groans as it heaves itself high above the world. It is calling us by our names, as it has called us by our names forever. We answer it back with the joy of recognition.

Until finally we find a forlorn little park. There's a little stone statue of an angel ringed in concrete and some pathetic little trees cornered by concrete between the benches, and the park is surrounded on all its sides by five massive, ancient trees whose mighty roots have raised the concrete around them so that the earth here looks fractured.

"Let's drink," I say. I know it will call me to myself still more. I grasp the cool bottle in Ham's hand. I bid Wally with that hand to do as I do: to drink, to forget one self and remember another.

"I don't remember much of those years after I left your house," I tell Wally. This is true for Ham. He tries not to let his recollection too near those years: not because there's something there he's specifically afraid of, but because he's afraid to see the yawning hole, spanning years, in his memory. He would rather skirt the edges, pick up the pieces scattered there and use them toward his own ends.

"But can I tell you what I do remember? I know it sounds strange."

"With you, anything goes."

"I lived in Peru."

"Sure you did."

"I swear I did. I swear by my mother."

"What mother?"

"You think I'm just motherless, don't you? But my mother was a beautiful woman. Dark. And fresh. The sun loved her face."

"Sure it did."

I let the gap in the teeth of Ham's remembered mother fill with the ivory brilliance of my own mother's mouth, and I staunch the bleeding gums. "Anyway, they say I got a baby," I continue, "in Alabama."

"Who say?"

"It's true though."

"How old?"

"Not born, I don't think."

"The mother?"

"Some girl."

Wally laughs. Wally the lady-killer. Wally who jumps into women to suck the poison out, who heals and discards them.

"Do you have kids?" I ask.

"No way," Wally says. "Not me. Not that I know of."

"Never?"

"One day maybe. I know it's what you're supposed to do. Just somehow I don't quite see it for myself."

I remember the wad of cash in the front pocket of Ham's backpack. Hundreds of dollars in twenty-dollar bills, some still stiff, some softened by the oil of countless hands and the anxious tremblings of countless fingers. I feel the mass of paper bills, pat it secure, then ask Wally, "How did you come to this town again?"

"My car," Wally says. "I've been driving all this way."

"What do you think about taking a detour from California?"

"There has to be a really good reason, Ham. Not just for anything."

"It's a good reason. We'll meet the baby."

Even Ham knows it's almost time now. Though it's Deborah's brother Ellis who has to take her to the hospital and though she has to lie alone there in the mechanical bed, fertile in a land of sterility, as Ellis leaves to fill out her paperwork. Though she has only the grit of her teeth to comfort her as the time draws near and though baby Margaret May claws at her in every last effort to maintain her place there in the womb—realizing in terror that the thing there is most of to grasp is water, and that even that slips through fingers (the body's first lessons now dawning in an apocalyptic epiphany), realizing that the rope she has to grasp is not only made of flesh like her, but that it has surrendered its anchor to her mother and is being pulled like everything else in the world she has known down the drain hole, into which the atmosphere itself—water, just water—is also sucked out, collapsing her mother's flesh around Margaret May's flesh in what feels like the clench of death.

Red and bawling, Margaret May is cleaned by the sterile hands of doctors who do not even know her mother's name, viewing both mother and new daughter as numbered viscera, the person reduced to an assignment, the giving of life reduced to a routine.

I cannot help but to take Ham's mind there when I travel, and in his memory there is the flash of Deborah's agonized face, her solitude in this hour of need tolling like a bell that calls him home. What is it there inside him when he thinks of her? Is it love? Born of obligation maybe but become love. Certainly.

"It's hard to say no to that," Wally says of Ham's suggestion that the two of them drive to Deborah's from here. "But I need a job bad."

"You need to go home. That's what you need."

"It ain't nothing there, Ham. Nothing there. The town is gutted."

"We'll find something. We'll baptize the baby. And find your mother."

"So you do have some sound ideas in that head of yours after all," Wally says.

"Yes, I swear I do."

Ham and Wally gather themselves. They pass the pharmacy, where Ham now remembers that he could stand to gather some things for the baby and for the journey. He doesn't want to go in there now, wants that door locked against him. They will have to stop later, and again a few hours later. They find Wally's car parked behind the pharmacy and throw themselves into it.

Ham has the feeling in him that he wants to gather all the righteous ones in the world to him and nestle in their hands, and he hopes he is on his way to doing that. One at a time; it will start with his baby, whose soul has never known a blemish. He doesn't think it's beyond him to track down the little sister he'd loved and been separated from as a boy and know her to be part of the tribe he will gather made of all who've been right and true by him. And somewhere in himself, in the heroic part, he wants to drive to that farm somewhere outside Dallas where the others are no doubt working their rows and scoop Gomez and Diego, take them with him to see his baby. But he can't; he'd severed his ties to them like the sinner he was and was always going to be. The best he could hope for from now on was to do right by himself and those who dared love him. He hadn't told any one of the other workers he's leaving. He knows it's a betrayal. Betrayal and love are mixed for Ham.

When they stop at a superstore on the way he chooses only the most beautiful things for his baby. Yellow things: a bib, tiny socks, a miniature wool blanket with lavender-colored flowers on it. Some big plastic toys she can slobber on.

Ham buys white cardboard boxes so he can bind everything up nicely, and he buys a spool of purple ribbon. In the parking lot, nursing one of the beers from the pack he bought that morning, he spreads everything on the blue metal hood of Wally's car, a surface that nearly scalds him with all the sun's heat it has been collecting over the course of the day. He ties everything nicely together. He places the blanket in its box last. And looking down at the package he feels unsatisfied. He clasps the pendant at his neck where he keeps my relic. He throws it down and tucks it into the blanket. This is the greatest portion of Margaret May's inheritance from him: a saint to guard and guide her.

Happily, Ham and Wally take up the things from the hood and put them neatly into the trunk. Then they ride out, onward toward the newborn child and the hope born with her.

8. In which Ham loses another ghost

Ham soon realizes that for Wally this journey is a kind of atone-
ment. In going to claim and care for Ham's baby girl, he is
checking karmic scales of a sort, making sure for himself that
any mistakes he might have made over the past few years are settled. His enthusiasm over the task of delivering Margaret May
Holmes her father is unmatched by anything Ham has previously
seen from Wally, with the possible exception of that one time
Wally made shortstop on the baseball team he played on as a kid
and threw himself wholeheartedly into the task of playing the
best he could, drawing outlines and diagrams of future games on
the napkins at Miss Pearl's table while Ham sat in the chair next
to him.

Ham remembers Atlanta on the drive. He remembers how
once in his endless wandering he rode the train to the end of

the western MARTA line and was surprised to see that the station there bore his own name. Landing there, he rode the elevator that was ripe with the smell of human piss, then he took the escalator back up, feeling he'd reclaimed some essential part of himself, and sat on the granite bench to catch the train back home to Mayfly again. It didn't make that city home for him, but it did give him the feeling that the city was his own. It let him feel in command of his life there to an extent. Now he was hoping he could gather this same feeling from the entire world as he moved through it.

I was thinking rare, hopeful thoughts.

I can't remember all the things I've been. Sometimes there's a glimmer of faraway places I've never been to, or faraway times. Where does it come from? In the first hours of their drive I'd felt suffocated by the baby's blanket around my bone, felt choked by the heat and warmth of being enclosed. Gradually I begin to loosen, unloosen, unsettle.

Ellis answered the phone when Ham had called to let them know he was on the way, and Ham heard the hurt defense in his tone. Surely they all hated him by now. Arthur probably always had, and he was surely gloating all over the two houses where he made his life. Bo was his friend, he knew that. Bo would always be his friend. Bo was probably helping to make things light for everyone, trying to light up the dark spaces Ham had opened in the home and the dark spaces within Deborah that threatened her health and the health of their child.

Theirs. It is the first time I allow myself to consider this child mine too.

"Ellis? It's Ham," he had said on the phone.

"Well now, that's someone whose voice I haven't heard in a while."

"Yes. I've missed everybody. I'm coming to visit. I'm an hour down the road now."

"We'll be ready."

"I hope it's alright if I take the baby out with me. I can have her back."

"She's a month old, Ham."

"We were thinking about some kind of a maybe low-key kind of baptism for her back home."

"She's going to be baptized here. It's already settled."

"At least we can show the baby to the family of my best friend from when I was a kid." Ham wasn't sure if he could call what people he has in his hometown through Wally his family.

"You have some nerve."

"I didn't mean to upset you."

"We'll just . . . we'll just see what everybody says. And we'll see how things go."

Through Mississippi their increasing distance from the water begins to show in the landscape. The palms become pines, the earth shifts from sandy and wet and black to thick red clay that holds water as perfectly as the vessels the first people to live on this land crafted from it.

They pull into the Everetts' driveway in the early afternoon, crackling the gravel underneath the car's tires. Ham goes up the stoop to the door that is only used for company, that enters into the salon where even company sit on plastic covers over the furniture. Everyone who is part of the daily life of the Everetts' household enters through the back door, the one leading into the yellow kitchen. But he will have to work his way back to that door. He looks over to the car and sees Wally going to the trunk and beginning to lift the packages they had placed there. The door is answered by Bo, cheerful and good-natured as always, or at least not revealing anything else beneath a calm face.

Ham remembers now, sliding on his jeans on the plastic furniture covers in the Everetts' salon, that it might have been good for him to bring some kind of jacket or overshirt. The way they keep the house air-conditioned is too much for him. Ham is not the type who needs more than a fan in the window even in summer. His blood is too warm, or else too cold.

Deborah's mother Azalea had returned to help take care of the baby and to be useful around the house, in all her glory. She wears platform shoes, spandex tights, and a loose T-shirt, extending a hand with long, sharp, red-lacquered nails to Ham in greeting. She smiles her disgust at him through painted lips. Cordial, but clearly she is not fond of what she knows of Ham. She doesn't have to be, Ham reckons to himself.

Now in their front room, Ellis takes Ham a cool glass of water. Ham feels wary of the water—like he can't be quite sure of the gifts Ellis is bearing him just yet. So he hands the glass to Wally beside him and gets up himself to fill a new glass with the well water the house uses from the kitchen sink. He drinks this sitting next to Wally, and it draws a calm and a cool and a patience to him.

"It's important to me to introduce her to my family. Not family exactly. I've never had family I guess, not really. Wally's people are the people that I know. Some folks are having a cookout, we can introduce her to her kin for the first time. Not kin, but. Something hasn't been the same since I left. To be able to show my daughter my world, what's left of it."

"We understand it's important to you," Ellis says, almost to keep Ham from going on and dipping into a well of emotion that would be uncomfortable for the both of them.

"It won't be like a fancy baptism. Just a gathering. People at gatherings always love babies."

"If it's important to you, you'll take the responsibility seriously and you won't let a hair on that baby's head be harmed in your sight. And you'll have her back in time."

"And it will give people there hope to see her. People waiting for the ones they've lost to return, people waiting for Wally's mother, Miss Pearl."

Soon enough, Deborah comes into the salon. The month-old baby's head rests in the nook between her neck and right shoulder and she supports the child's weight in her arms. She makes baby Margaret May look like the lightest burden, a perfect parcel.

"We call her Maggie," she says to Ham, carefully taking a seat with babe in arms on the armchair next to them. She squeaks the plastic cover slightly with the motion of her body.

"I'm glad to see you came back, Ham," she tells him.

"I'm glad to be back. You know I'd never leave you and her alone."

"Yeah, you told me that once. I pretty much knew better than to believe you."

The baby starts to fuss at these words. "Here," Deborah says, lightly lifting herself from the seat to place Maggie in Ham's arms. He fixes his arms at still right angles to receive Margaret May, like a robot, and a tiny fear that he can't care for her right takes hold of him and causes his arms to shake a little.

"Don't worry, she's not heavy," Deborah tells him.

The weight of his child sends a current of calm into Ham. This is a calm he's never known before and so he is in awe of it—of the calm, of the baby, of her mother, of the forgiveness he's not even sure he deserves yet is already there.

"Ham, can we talk?" Deborah asks.

"About what?" Ham says dumbly.

"About everything."

Ham sighs. "Maybe when I get back?"

"Okay."

Wally crosses the room to where they are. He feels it's his place to speak, maybe noticing a skepticism in Arthur's brow. "We'll have her home just after dark, don't worry."

"Oh, I don't worry none. You can't worry, with this one," she says, cocking her head in Ham's direction. "If you choose to worry more than an instant you'll go mad, the things he do."

"But they're all alright when it's said and done," Ham says. He speaks the words over the baby's head. They are a prayer: words he doesn't always believe that some other part of him holds and assuredly carries to fruition. The words give him enough hope to continue.

"I wish I could tell you how important it is and how glad I am that you would trust me." He is lucky he has me in this moment to steady his limbs, so he doesn't betray the emotion straining inside him with any movement.

"You don't have to, Ham. You've never been good at this. When you come back, you will."

Hearing them, Deborah's brother Arthur interjects with a wheeze, "He can explain. It's the least he can do."

"I guess it's like . . . I have to gather everything good to me and place it next to everything that used to be good, back home."

"And then?" Arthur presses. "Maybe everything doesn't belong in that world. The baby belongs right here."

"Maybe she won't belong there, maybe I won't belong there either. I have to at least find out. It will be good for her to know that part of her, and I'll have her back soon." It may be the most he's ever said to Arthur, and the words leave him breathless.

They all enjoy a late breakfast in the kitchen, Deborah, Ellis, Bo, Ham, Wally, and Azalea, after Arthur excused himself to go home. The house is warming up to him again. He can tell just by the fact that he's allowed to move within the kitchen like he lives here, opening the drawers himself to easily find the forks and set them out for everyone.

From his side-eye Ham watches the child who sits in a baby seat in the corner, a seat that's on rockers so she can rest calmly, above which the rainbow of a mobile arcs with bright and shining plastic objects that can keep the child entertained as she practices her new eyesight on them, fascinated by distance, by shape, by form, by proximity to objects and people. Ham has noticed that his baby's mouth is a perfect puckered raisin. Everything about her is perfect, like it's been formed of porcelain, painted a delicate brown, and glazed to shine.

Deborah feeds the child from her breast after the meal. She takes from the refrigerator two bottles filled with her milk, and she gives those to Wally, who puts them in the car. The gifts for the child lie heaped in the salon like Christmas.

Ham will hold the child the whole way to his hometown as Wally steers the car with an easy hand. Ham is sure of what he's doing. He's never been surer about what he's doing. About fifteen minutes into the trip, they pass the lake again, the lake Ham had noticed first the last time he left the house and then noticed when passing again on the way in. Now the lake is covered in a blanket of green, algae and pollen resting on the water's surface in the creator's exacting portions.

They all ride in near silence. Sometimes the baby coos, sometimes Ham shushes, and sometimes Wally goes, "Do-do-do," quietly tracing some tune that echoes in his head. Then Wally says, "That baby's never going back, is she?"

Ham laughs. "You never know."

In only a few hours they have neared his hometown, and the plants along the highway are familiar to Ham's blood. We are home. At three in the afternoon the sun sits like a glowing ember perched at the top of the sky's second-to-last quarter, and

Wally and Ham have reached the bridge over the Pontchartrain in Wally's blue car that reflects the sun's light like the hard shell of a scarab. Surely Mayfly awaits them in the city, as do countless wonders. She didn't mean what she said. Ham imagines himself meeting Mayfly at a barbeque in one of the city's swampy wards. Imagines introducing the baby to her, handing the child to her, and Mayfly reacting with grace. He knows that everything is well between them. The sky is blue, blue, blue.

Now inside their car, baby Margaret May lies curled at Ham's chest, drooling the most delicate thread of saliva, thin as a spider's woven strand, down her cotton onesie, dampening both her clothes and her father's.

On impulse Ham reaches into the back seat, into the baby's car seat, to grab the blanket with my pendant in it. He rolls down his window, removes the pendant, and throws it out. It sails silver into the sky, reaches over the lake where it will find its home among the fish. The object has done its work, fulfilled the mission Pearl had first assigned it: it's brought Ham home. His body is his now; he'll see after himself and ready himself to see after someone else for a change. I am overcome by saltwater. This is what Ham wants, to be his own.

Outside the car windows the water glimmers, and they in their vehicle slide into a wet cloak of fog that mists their view a little, and this air ferries them into the city's warm and waiting folds. Rise up, it commands, measuredly.

I want to obey, to rise and find an easy home with Ham. To be near him as the car winds through the city's suburbs, lush and wild, and the air that can't keep from flooding the car with smells of sweet rot and the ocean, the unmistakable scents from Ham's childhood stronger and more overpowering than he'd ever known them, fully blooming in this wake since catastrophe and swelling his senses. It's a sure sign that they're approaching home. He's already decided that whatever stands, his remembrance stands, and that's what guides him past these narrow wooden houses he knew, some hollowed out in the disaster nearly a year ago, some grotesquely marked with spray paint to indicate the living and the dead, to separate out what needs saving. It's midafternoon and Wally in the passenger seat has nodded to sleep and the sun slides down the electrical wires that crisscross above the flat streets. A familiar corner store comes up on the left, and Ham waves at the clerk leaning against the doorframe of the building whose windows have now been boarded up, not knowing if he's recognized. Now, as he touches home, Ham sees that patching things together for himself, building a world for this baby, is only the beginning. He considers, too, that maybe better than having Mayfly, better than chasing her or hoping for her to be around the corner, is doing as she does and letting go. Considering her one of the ones reclaimed by the water and gathering what's left before it's washed away. And saltwater overwhelms me, water becomes my new host, until I can rise, until I can find a home in new bones.

ACKNOWLEDGMENTS

Deep love to all the ancestors whose blood runs through me and who empower me. Thank you to everyone I've known in Atlanta and everyone who guided me through New Orleans over the years, including Gloria Gayles of the SIS project, Natalie Kuhl, and Kara Gionfriddo. Gratitude to Linda Janet Holmes for believing and encouraging always, and for guiding me to my work. Thank you to Frank Reiss of A Cappella Books for giving me space to write, and to the writers of the Verbalists for support. Thanks to the Vermont Studio Center for hosting me at the residency that allowed me to write the first bulk of this book, and to all the beautiful artists whose lives and work inspired me there. Thanks to my mother, Janine Rouson, my sister Maryann James-Daley, and Andrea Stroud for early reads. Thank you to Annie Wheliss for helping to resurrect the book when it needed it, and to my agent Stephanie Delman for her faith. Gratitude for my editor Jenny Alton's truly seeing the book. Thanks to cover designer Dana Li, creative director Nicole Caputo, production editor and book designer Jordan Koluch, managing editor Wah-Ming Chang, copy editor Sue Ducharme, editorial assistant Yukiko Tominaga, publicist Selihah White, director of publicity Megan Fishmann, events and marketing manager Katie Boland, events and marketing assistant Samm Saxby, executive director of marketing Rachel Fershleiser, social media editor Dustin Kurtz, publishing operations associate Miyako Singer, and the whole team at Counterpoint who helped this book come to be.

© Zoë Davidson

CHANTAL JAMES lives in Washington, D.C., and has been published across genres—as a poet, fiction writer, essayist, and book reviewer—in such venues as *Catapult*, *Paste*, Harvard's *Transition*, *The Bitter Southerner*, and more. James's honors include a Fulbright Fellowship in creative writing to Morocco and a finalist position for the Alex Albright Creative Nonfiction Prize from the North Carolina Literary Review in 2019.